High Maintenance

Fernandina Beach Mysteries

High Maintenance

By

Rodney Riesel

Published by Island Holiday Publishing
East Greenbush, NY

Copyright © 2018 Rodney Riesel

All rights reserved

ISBN: 978-1-7324257-4-3

First Edition

This is a work of fiction. Names, characters, businesses, places, events, and incidents either are the product of the author's imagination or are used fictitiously. Any resemblance to actual persons, living or dead, events or locales is purely coincidental.

Special thanks to:

Pamela Guerriere

Kevin Cook

Cover Image by:

www.123rf.com/jovannig

Cover Design by:

Connie Fitsik

To learn about my other books friend me at

https://www.facebook.com/rodneyriesel

**For Brenda,
Kayleigh, Ethan
& Peyton**

Chapter One

It was Tuesday morning when I dropped Gayle off at Brett's Waterway Cafe, where she works part-time as a waitress. Her car was in the shop, so I would be picking her up after work as well. I didn't mind, as I didn't have much else to do. I used to own a small construction company, but I sold it a few years back when I retired, and now I work part-time as a maintenance man at Collins' Hardware.

Collins' Hardware is a family-owned and operated store in Fernandina Beach, on Amelia Island in Northeast Florida. The hardware store is on the first floor of a four-story brick building on Centre Street. I fix pretty much anything that needs fixing or remodeling in the store, and in the apartments on the three floors above.

I pulled my '94 Ford F-150 to the curb in front of Amelia Island Coffee and went inside for a cup to go.

Like most mornings, Janice Godfrey was behind the counter wearing a white apron with her jet-black hair pulled into a tight bun on top of her head. Janice was in her mid-sixties, but there wasn't a streak of gray on that head.

"Good morning, Rex," said Janice.

"Morning, Janice," I replied. I glanced around the room at the few patrons seated at small round tables. The only one I recognized was Lloyd Cushing.

"Mornin', Rex," Lloyd said.

"Morning, Lloyd." Whenever I spoke to Lloyd I tried my hardest to keep eye contact, but my focus always landed on that off-colored front tooth of his. All of his teeth seemed to be normal color and size, except for that one grayish-brown tooth. It was longer—and even wider—than the others. I always felt as though I was speaking to his tooth. I wondered if other people did the same. I also wondered if he noticed when I was staring at that damn thing.

"The usual?" Janice asked.

"Please," I replied. I turned back to the counter and away from that damn tooth.

Janice poured the coffee, black with no sugar, and placed it on the counter in front of me.

I tossed a five and three ones onto the counter and said, "Thanks, Janice. Keep the change."

"Thanks, Rex," she said, and dropped the change into a glass tip jar next to the register.

As I walked next door to the hardware store, I removed the lid of my cup and blew into the steaming hot coffee. I tried to take a little sip, but it was just too hot. I blew into it again and put the lid back on.

I grabbed the handle on the entrance door and pulled it open for the elderly customer who was backing through it. He had four gallons of paint in a cardboard box and was pushing open the door with his butt.

"Here, let me get that for you," I said.

"Thanks, that's most kind of you," said the old guy.

I held the door until he was through and heading down the street to his car. "You have a nice day," I said.

"You do the same, young man."

Ha! Young man, I thought. *What a great way to start the day*. I'm not really a young man. I'm forty-eight. But hey, who doesn't want to hear it any way, even if it is coming from an old fossil.

I went inside. Christine, Kevin's sister, was behind the checkout counter. Kevin's son, Mark, was on the phone.

"Kevin around?" I asked.

Kevin Collins had been the owner of Collins' Hardware for around ten years, since his father passed away.

"He just went to breakfast," Christine replied.

"Okay," I said. "I'm going to head upstairs and put that new doorknob on thirty-four. Did he mention if there was anything else?"

Christine thought for a second. "Yeah, he did mention something else." she said, as she remained in deep thought.

"What was it?" I asked.

"I can't remember. I'll have him call you when he gets back. He should be back in a half hour or so."

"Sounds good." I hung a left at the end of the checkout counter and a quick right down the aisle with doorknobs. About halfway down I stopped in front of the entry lock sets. The cheapest one was twelve bucks; I grabbed it.

Christine scanned the bar code on my way out and told me to have fun.

I replied, "Always do," and went out the door.

An alleyway runs down the right-hand side of the building. Halfway down the building there's an entrance door that leads to a long hallway. At the end of that hall is an elevator. There's also a door on Centre Street, just to the left of the hardware store's entrance. That door leads to a staircase that winds around and up all four floors. I don't take the stairs very often.

The elevator doors parted, and I stepped off onto the fourth floor. The doorknob I was changing is on the third, but I keep my tools in a small store room on the fourth. I unclipped the key ring that hangs on my belt loop and searched for the key with the purple tag; all the keys are colored and numbered.

I grabbed my drill, an extension cord, and the black canvas bag full of my drill bits. I returned to the third floor and walked up to the door of apartment thirty-two. I gave the door a couple raps with my knuckles and waited. About thirty seconds later I knocked again.

Apartment thirty-two belonged to Cruz Salas and his wife, Frankie; they were in their early fifties. Cruz drives tractor-trailer, and is gone a lot. Frankie keeps house, goes shopping, has lunch with friends, and spends most of her evenings in local bars. I've seen Detective Rance's nephew, Donny, coming out of her apartment in the morning on two different occasions. I haven't mentioned anything to Rance. I don't know if I should. On one hand, the kid is bangin' someone else's wife. On the other hand, lucky bastard.

I knocked for the third time. Kevin had told me he would call and let Frankie know I would be coming, but I was starting to think he had forgotten. I pulled out my cell phone and called downstairs.

"Collins' Hardware," Christine announced.

"Chris, it's Rex. Can you call Frankie Salas and see if she's around? Kevin was supposed to call yesterday. She's not answering her door."

"Sure thing," said Christine, and hung up.

I gave the door another rap, just for good measure, and put my tools on the floor. I leaned my back against the wall and waited.

I thought about Edgar Hayes, and how I had walked into his apartment a month earlier and found him lying dead on his kitchen floor. I hoped I wasn't about to walk in on Frankie Salas the same way. It's funny, before I walked in on Edgar and saw him lying there like that, I never expected to find a dead person in an apartment. Now, since that day, I expect it almost every time I walk into one. I wondered how long I would feel that way. I figured I would probably experience that feeling right up until the day before it happened again.

I heard movement in the apartment and pushed myself away from the wall. The door opened. Frankie looked rough.

"Morning, Frankie," I said.

She was squinting as though I was shining a floodlight in her face. "Morning, Rex," she said through morning phlegm, then cleared her throat. "I didn't hear you knocking. I sleep with a fan on."

"Did Kevin tell you I was coming this morning?"

"No," she replied. "But Christine just called to let me know."

"You want me to come back later?"

She pulled the door open the rest of the way. "No, that's fine, sweetheart. You come on in."

Frankie's long red hair was sticking out in every direction, and her bedroom eyes, though puffy from sleep and makeup-smear, still managed to look sexy. She was wearing a man's blue flannel robe that she was holding closed with her clenched hand. I had to wonder if she was completely naked under there. It's in my contract as a red-blooded American Male.

"Rough night?" I asked.

She pushed her hair out of her face and grinned; she had beautiful teeth. "You should see the other guy," she said. She stepped back and I entered.

"What seems to be the problem with this thing?" I asked.

"It locks and unlocks from inside the apartment, but when the door is closed, I can't unlock it from outside with my key."

"Okay," I responded. "I'm just going to put a new one on."

"Thanks." Frankie turned and walked back down the hall. She looked good from behind.

"I'm gonna make myself a cup of coffee. You want one?" she asked.

"I just finished a cup, but thanks." I took a Phillips screwdriver out of the drill bag and began removing the knob.

After Frankie had poured her cup of coffee, she came back down the hall. "Sure you don't want a cup, Rex?" she asked.

"I'm sure," I said.

Frankie continued to watch over my shoulder as I removed the cylinder and opened the new package. I wondered if she would stand there the entire time. I always found it funny that people would stand over me while I worked and watch my every move. It used to happen all the time back before I sold my construction business. I can remember old, retired men and women standing in a room I was working in all day and watch as I sheetrocked, or did whatever else I had to do. At least now that I was just a maintenance man, the jobs didn't take as long.

Just as I was finishing up, the elevator doors opened, and Donny Rush stepped onto the floor. I could tell by the look in his eyes that he was surprised to see me. "Um ... h-hey," he stuttered. "What's up, Mr. Langley?"

"Not much, Donny," I said. "What's up with you?"

"Nothin'."

Donny Rush was Detective Calvin Rance's nephew; his sister's kid. He was twenty-seven years old. He was tall and thin, like his uncle Calvin. Donny had moved into Edgar Hayes's old apartment on the second floor a couple weeks earlier.

Donny's eyes rose and he looked past me. "Hey, Frankie," he said. His face flushed.

"Morning, sweetheart," Frankie replied.

I wanted to turn around and see what kind of a look Frankie had on her face, but didn't want to appear too obvious. Also, I was a little disappointed that Frankie seemed to call everyone sweetheart. I thought it was just me.

"Did you need to borrow a cup of sugar or something, sweetheart?" Frankie asked.

I knew Frankie was just ribbing the kid.

"Yeah, Donny," I said. "You come up for some of Frankie's sugar?"

Frankie nudged me in the back with her knee.

Donny's face turned even redder. "No ... I, uh," he said. "I was looking for you actually."

I dropped my screwdriver back into the drill bag and zipped it closed. "Oh yeah?" I asked. "You weren't looking for some of my sugar, I hope."

Donny grinned nervously. "No."

"What did you need?" I asked, as I wound my extension cord around my arm.

"You know that lady in apartment twenty-three?" he asked.

"Robin?"

"Yeah."

"What about her?"

"I haven't seen her in a few days."

"So? I haven't seen her in, like, two weeks." I picked up my drill and drill bag and stepped out into the hall.

"Seriously, Mr. Langley. I see her almost every day, and now haven't seen her since Wednesday, I think."

"Maybe she went on a trip or something," I offered. "I wouldn't worry about it if I were you."

"Her car is still out in the parking lot," Donny informed me.

"Maybe she rode with someone else."

"She didn't mention she was going anywhere."

Frankie cut in. "I'm going to shut the door," she said. "Stop over later if you want, Donny."

"Okay, Mrs. Salas," he replied.

She shut the door and I cocked my head. "Mrs. Salas?" I snorted. "Who do you think you're fooling with that Eddie Haskell routine?"

High Maintenance

"I don't know what you mean, Mr. Langley."

"Sure you don't." I turned and headed for the elevator.

Donny followed. "What are you going to do about Robin?"

I stepped onto the elevator and so did Donny. "Nothing," I said.

"She has a dog."

"So?"

"What if it hasn't eaten?"

"Have you heard it barking?"

"No."

"Then she probably took it with her."

The doors parted on the second floor and Donny stepped off. "Yeah, maybe," he responded.

The doors closed again and I checked my watch. *Awesome*, I thought. *I'll be home in time for Days of Our Lives.*

Chapter Two

I drove over the railroad tracks, took a right onto Front Street, and pulled into the parking lot next to Brett's Waterway Cafe, where Gayle had been working as a waitress part-time for over four years.

When I met Gayle she was thirty years old, and I was thirty-four. She had a thirteen-year-old son at the time named Ben. Gayle had Ben when she was seventeen, and enlisted in the Navy a year later. Ben lived with his grandparents—his biological father's parents—in Boston until he was six years old, and then went to live with Gayle in San Diego. Gayle was stationed in San Diego for the first ten years and was then transferred to Naval Station Mayport in Jacksonville, where she spent the remainder of her military career. I adopted Ben and gave him my last name soon after Gayle and I were married. Ben never knew his real father; he was killed in a car accident when Ben was only one.

I walked along the brick sidewalk to the steps that lead to the deck that surrounds Brett's Waterway Cafe. I grabbed a seat at a small table in the rear that overlooks the boat docks and the Amelia River. There was a slight breeze coming off the water, and the sun was hiding behind the clouds. I wished I had worn a long-sleeved shirt.

Gayle was waiting on a four top a few feet away from me; she hadn't seen me yet. I turned my chair slightly so I could gawk at the tourists as they made their way along the boardwalk. I watched a young couple as they stopped and pointed at the sterns of several boats, reading their names. The guy took out his cell phone and snapped a picture of a sailboat puckishly named BEST DIVORCE LAWYER EVER.

After Gayle finished taking the four top's order, I said, "Excuse me, ma'am."

She spun around and gave me the stink eye. "Ma'am?" she said, her voice thick with umbrage.

"Uh … miss?"

"That's better," she said. "You're early."

"I needed a drink."

"Why, what happened now?"

"Hope told Rafe she wants to have their marriage annulled. Rafe told her—"

Gayle waived me off. "You're an idiot," she said, and spun on her heels.

For a second I wondered if that meant I wasn't getting my drink, but she returned a few minutes later with a Bacardi and ginger ale and placed it on the table in front of me.

"Here you go," said Gayle. "And I expect a tip."

"Tip? Hell, I'll give you the whole thi—"

"Shut up." She walked to another table and pulled out her check pad.

High Maintenance

I sipped my drink and returned my attention to the tourists passing by. The variety of humankind in a beach town never ceases to amaze me. I'm always reminded of the famous illustration *The Road to Homo Sapiens*, depicting human evolution from knuckle-dragging ape to upright-walking man. Having spent untold hours people-gazing all over Amelia Island, I'm convinced the artist must have done his research right here, as I've observed every phase of hominid and human represented in the drawing. Don't get me wrong, there are some beautiful people here, including the bodacious bikinied beach bunnies that make me wish Fernandina was clothing-optional. Unfortunately, there are also male and female missing links that should never be allowed to get nekkid in public—unless everybody else on the beach has been issued red-hot pokers with which to gouge out their eyes.

Forty-five minutes passed with excruciating slowness. Gayle had come by my table to inform me her shift was about over. Meanwhile I watched another missing link stroll down the boardwalk. He was as white as a beached manatee, just as fat, and in desperate need of a bra. He was wearing tiny Speedos from which the twin moons of his ass spilled out like two plates of cottage cheese. He idly licked an ice cream cone as the breeze stirred the forest of kinky black hair on his shoulders and back. The man could have carried his pendulous belly in a wheelbarrow. I lost my appetite for the fried green tomatoes appetizer I had considered ordering.

Gayle's shift was finally over. She came over, gave me a kiss, and sat down next to me.

"Have you ever noticed," I said dryly, "that the people who shouldn't be parading around in next to nothing, are always the ones that do?"

Gayle nodded knowingly. "People watching again?"

"Yeah. Got a red-hot poker, by any chance?"

Gayle gave me the doe caught in the headlights look. "Never mind," I said.

I had nursed my drink down to a little bit of melted ice.

"Are you going to have a drink?" I asked.

"Not here," she said. "I can't relax here. I feel like I should be working.

"That's fine." I got up and so did Gayle.

"I already paid for your drink," she said.

"Big spender," I said.

We walked to my truck and pulled out of the parking lot.

"Did you want to go somewhere for a drink?" I asked. "Or did you just want to go home."

"Let's just go home," Gayle replied. "I'm tired."

"Your wish is my command."

"Awesome. I wish … you would make dinner tonight."

"How about if we stop somewhere and grab something to take home?"

"Sounds good."

"Chinese?"

"That sounds good."

"Lucky Wok?" I suggested.

"New China." Gayle decided.

Gayle called in our order from the truck and when we got there we only had about ten minutes to wait. New China is located in the Amelia Plaza Shopping Center,

High Maintenance

right between Walmart and Winn-Dixie. We remained in my truck in the parking lot and waited.

"How was work?" Gayle asked.

"I replaced a door knob," I replied.

"That's it?"

"Yup."

"How long did that take?"

"Twenty minutes."

"So you only worked for twenty minutes today?'

"Yup."

"Must be nice."

"Kevin didn't have anything else for me to do."

Gayle looked at her watch. "Five more minutes."

"There's a couple on the fourth floor moving out next week," I said. "I have to paint the entire place. That should take a couple weeks."

"You'll probably have to DVR your soaps," Gayle joked.

"It's one soap," I defended.

"Did you get Edgar's apartment all rented out?"

"Yup. Rance's nephew moved in a couple weeks ago. He was supposed to find a roommate to help him with the rent, but he never did. I don't know how he's going to afford the place. And, I think he's got something going on with a married woman in the building."

"Something going on?" Gayle asked. "You mean they're screwing?"

"Yup."

"You can say screwing. We're both adults here."

"I was trying to make it sound better than it was."

"Who is it?"

"Frankie Salas."

"The red head?"

"Yup."

"Huh. How old is she?"

"Fifty something."

"How old's the kid?"

"Twenty-seven."

"Sounds like a match made in heaven."

"He also thinks another woman in the building has disappeared."

"He bangin' that broad as well?" Gayle asked.

Sometimes when Gayle and I had conversations it almost felt like I was talking to another dude. I always chalked that up to the fact that she was a military cop for twenty years.

"I don't think he is."

"Who is she?"

"Her name's Robin Day. She moved in a couple months before Donny—that's Rance's nephew."

"How old's Robin?"

"Probably around the same age as Donny."

"Way too young for him then. She live alone?"

"She has a dog."

"But no roommate?"

"Nope."

"How long she been missing?"

"She's not missing."

"How do you know?"

"She probably just went on a trip or something."

"Probably," Gayle said. She looked at her watch again. "Go see if the food's ready."

I saluted. "Yes, ma'am."

"Miss."

"Yes, miss doesn't sound right with a salute."

Chapter Three

On my way to work Wednesday morning Detective Calvin Rance called me. "Hello?" I said.

"Rex, it's Detective Rance," he said.

"Hey, pal! What's up?" Whenever Rance called me I always said, "Hey, pal!" with a lot more excitement than I was actually feeling. Mostly I did it because I knew we weren't really pals, and I knew it bugged him. I tried to be friends with Rance when I first met him a few weeks back, but he wasn't very receptive. He seemed like a nice guy and I thought it was pretty cool that he was a police detective. Gayle says I have a man crush on him. I think Gayle is just jealous because Rance is cooler than her. I figure if I keep calling him pal, I can wear him down.

"We're not pals," he said.

"Ha!," I said. "What a kidder."

"Yeah. Anyway, the reason I'm calling is because my nephew called me last night and said there was a woman in his building that hasn't been home in a few nights."

"Yeah. Robin Day."

"Right. That's her. What's that all about?"

I pulled to the curb in front of Amelia Island Coffee and shut off my engine. "Donny said he hadn't seen her in a few days. He said she has a dog and he wondered if it was in the apartment. I asked him if he had heard a dog barking, and he said no. I told him she probably went on a trip or something."

"Donny said her car is still in the parking lot."

"Yeah, I figure she left with a friend."

"Can you get in her apartment?"

"I have a key."

"Will you go in and take a look around?"

"I'll have to ask Kevin if it's okay."

"That's fine."

"You want to be here when I go in?"

"No, I don't think so. Just let me know what you see."

"Okay. You have plans for lunch?"

"Nope."

"How about I meet you at the Crab Trap and we'll talk about it there."

"Sounds good," Rance said, and hung up.

I put my cell away, climbed out of the truck, and went into the coffee shop.

"Hey, Rex," Janice said.

"Hey, Janice," I replied. "Hey, Lloyd."

"The usual?" Janice asked.

"Yup."

High Maintenance

While pouring my coffee she said, "Hear we got a missing girl next door."

"How the hell did you hear that?" I asked.

"Heard she was abducted," said Lloyd. "What's the world comin' to?"

"No one was abducted," I said.

"Just missing?' asked Janice.

"No one is missing either."

Janice put the lid on my to-go cup and slid it over in front of me. "That's good," she said. "So you found her already?"

"She was never missing," I said.

"Tryin' to keep it hush-hush?" Lloyd asked.

I sighed. "Yeah, Lloyd. We're trying to keep it on the down low. Please don't mention it to anyone."

Lloyd winked, made a snapping noise with his tongue, and pointed at me. "You got it, Rex. You can trust me."

I paid and headed for the door. "Oh, I know I can, Lloyd. Thanks."

I walked out of Amelia Island Coffee and walked next door to Collins' Hardware. "Hey, Christine," I said.

"Morning, Rex," she replied.

"Kevin around?"

She scanned the area. "He's around here somewhere."

Kevin's office was in the basement. That's the first place I checked; he wasn't there. I walked out to the paint room. "Sal, you seen Kevin?"

Sal was mixing paint for a customer. "He's around here somewhere," he replied. Sal was a heavy set Italian guy, with black wavy hair and olive skin. Sal had worked for the Fernandina Department of Public Works for thirty years and came to work at the hardware store after he retired. Sal was around five-eight and in his mid-sixties, but looked much younger.

I checked the plumbing aisle next, and that's where I found Kevin. He was stocking the shelves with galvanized pipe fittings.

"What do we got today?" I asked.

"Can you put a couple of those LED fixtures over my work bench in the basement?" Kevin asked. "I'm getting so bad I can hardly see when I'm down there to sharpen saw blades."

"Sure," I said. "Come down with me so you can show me exactly where you want them."

I turned and Kevin followed me. Behind the checkout counter there was another set of stairs that led to the basement. This section of basement was separate from where Kevin kept his office. We walked down the stairs and around behind them to a workbench where Kevin sharpened saw blades, drill bits, chisels, and other pieces of metal that needed a sharp edge.

Kevin pointed at the ceiling. "Can you put one there, there, there, and there?"

"So, four of them?"

"Yeah."

"I can do that."

"And can you put them all on one switch at the top of the stairs?"

"Sure can," I replied. "But first, can I go in someone's apartment who isn't home?"

"For what?" Kevin asked.

High Maintenance

"Donny Rush says he hasn't seen Robin Day, in twenty-three, in a few days."

"So what?"

"He called Calvin Rance and told him. Rance wants me to go in and check it out, and let him know what I find."

"What will you be looking for?"

"I don't know."

"I guess you can go in. Just don't touch anything."

"I won't."

"I don't want her to know anyone was in there when she gets back."

"You got it," I said.

"Are you going to do these lights today?"

"Yup. I'll come down and start as soon as I have a look around her apartment."

I went back up the stairs and out the front door.

The elevator doors parted and I stepped off onto the second floor. I unclipped my key ring from my belt loop and started down the hall toward apartment twenty-three. When I got there, I gave it a couple raps, hoping someone would answer. As I slid the key into the lock and turned, visions of Edgar's lifeless body on his kitchen floor flashed into my mind. I cringed a little and the hair on my arms stood up. I pushed open the door, but stayed in the hall. I breathed in through my nose, wondering if a dead body would be stinking up the place within a few days. I couldn't smell anything so I went in.

"Robin?" I called out quietly. "Miss Day?" a little louder. "Is anyone here?"

Rodney Riesel

Robin Day's apartment was a one-bedroom with a living room and a large eat-in kitchen. The bedroom was across from her front door. I pushed it open and looked inside. I walked into her living room and then into the kitchen. There was no one in the apartment.

I glanced down at the two small stainless steel bowls on the kitchen floor next to the stove. Both bowls were empty. I turned around and looked back into the living room, and there on the couch was a black miniature poodle, so tiny and delicate and perfect it almost didn't look real. It just lay there staring at me. I followed my nose to a corner where the dog had crapped a couple times. He'd peed there, too, judging from the dark, irregular stain on the cheap carpet.

"Hey, there," I said. I walked closer; the puppy didn't move. I saw it blink, so I knew it wasn't dead. "Are you okay?" I was speaking quietly, the way someone would speak to a scared child. I knelt down in front of the puppy and put the back of my hand in front of its mouth. "Where's your mommy?"

The little guy sniffed and then licked the back of my hand. I ran my hand down his back. I could feel his bones. It was obvious he hadn't eaten in a few days. I returned to the kitchen and filled one of the bowls with water and held it at the edge of the couch in front of him. "Take a drink," I said.

The little fella lifted his head and his tongue shot in and out of his mouth, catching water with each lap. "Slow down," I warned. I didn't know if dogs were like people, and too much too soon would be bad for him. I set the bowl on the floor and went in search of food.

In the cupboard over the microwave there were a few cans of puppy food. I found a can opener and scooped about half the can into the other dish and brought it over to the dog. I spoke to him and questioned him about the disappearance of his owner as I put food on my fingertip and fed it to him. After feeding him about a quarter of what I had put in the dish, I gave him some more water, and called Gayle.

"Hey, you busy?" I asked when she answered. Gayle had the day off, so I knew she probably wasn't busy, but asking was a habit.

"Not really," she replied. "What's going on?"

"I'm in Robin Day's apartment."

"Okay."

"Rance called me this morning and wanted me to check it out."

"How did Rance hear about the situation?"

"Donny called him last night."

"Okay. Go on."

"She isn't here, her car is in the parking lot, and her dog is lying on the couch. He looks like he hasn't had any food or water in a couple of days."

"Strange."

"Yeah. Rance wanted me to look around."

"So, look around."

"What am I looking for?"

"Personal items," Gayle replied. "Look around the apartment. Did she leave her pocketbook behind? Are her suitcases still in her closet? Go in the bathroom. Is her toothbrush there? What about her blow dryer, curling iron, things like that? Is she a runner? Did she leave her running shoes behind? Women love to run on vacation."

"You're good at this," I said.

"Thanks," she replied.

I walked into the bedroom and opened the closet door. "There's no suitcases in here," I told Gayle. I walked to the bathroom. "Blow dryer is here." I opened the medicine chest. "I don't see a toothbrush. She must have taken it with her." I walked back into the kitchen and looked around. "I don't see a pocketbook anywhere."

"Sounds like she took everything she needed," Gayle offered.

"What about the dog, though," I asked. "Seems odd she would leave him behind."

"Maybe someone was supposed to be stopping over to feed him and forgot."

"Maybe." I walked back into the bedroom and opened a drawer in her dresser.

"What are you doing now?" Gayle asked.

"Looking through her drawers."

"For what?"

"I don't know. She has a lot of underwear." I held up a pair. "Thongs."

"What size?"

"Four. Why?"

"Just wondered."

"What are you?"

"It doesn't matter."

"Are you a four?"

"I'm a six, Rex."

I felt around underneath her panties and pulled something out. "What's this?" I asked, and then quickly dropped it.

"What was it?" Gayle asked.

"A sex thing," I replied.

"A sex thing? What kind of sex thing?"

"You know," I replied. "A sex ... *thing*."

"Oh, a sex thing. Is it a regular plastic vibrator, or does it look like a penis?"

"It's shaped just like a penis. Why, what are you thinking?"

"Nothing. Just being nosy. What color is it? And more importantly, how long is it?"

"Really, Gayle?" I placed some of the panties over Robin's dildo and closed the drawer. "Anything else I should look for?" I asked.

"Not that I can think of."

"Okay. Thanks for your help."

"Were we going to have lunch together?"

"I'm having lunch with Rance."

"Woo," said Gayle. "Lunch with your boyfriend."

"Shut up."

Gayle laughed, told me she loved me, and hung up. I locked up and headed back to the elevator.

Chapter Four

Rance and I took a seat at a four top at the Crab Trap. Rance won't sit at the bar if he's on duty. Why it matters where you sit is beyond me.

The Crab Trap is located in a two-story brick building at the corner of Second Street and Alachua Street. The interior walls are all exposed brick. Fishing nets and lobster and crab traps hang from the walls and ceiling. There's a couple blue marlins mounted on the walls: one at the west wall back near the bathrooms, and an even bigger one about half way down the east wall.

I ordered the fish burger and a beer, and Rance ordered the house salad with a side of fat-free dressing, and water.

"What are you, on some kind of diet or something?" I asked.

"No," Rance replied.

"How come you don't get a burger, or something?"

"Because I don't eat like that."

"You mean like a human?"

Rance shook his head as he ever so daintily dipped a piece of salad into the dressing. "What did you find out?" he asked.

"I went in and looked around for some personal items, like suitcases, a toothbrush—things she would have taken with her if she left voluntarily."

"Gayle tell you to do that?"

"What makes you ask that?"

"I can't imagine you thought of that on your own."

"Wow, thanks."

"You know what I mean."

"No, I don't. Anyway. Her toothbrush was gone. There were no suitcases in the apartment. Her pocketbook was gone too."

"So she probably did go on a trip," Rance surmised.

"Well, maybe, but her dog was in the apartment, and it looked as though it hadn't eaten in a few days."

"Maybe someone was supposed to stop over and feed it, but forgot."

"That's what Gayle said."

"So you did talk to Gayle. I knew it."

"Shut up."

"Where's the dog now?"

"I fed it and watered it. I'm going to go back to check on him after lunch."

"When was the last time you remember seeing—what's her name?"

"Robin ... Robin Day. And I couldn't tell you. It could have been two weeks since I've seen her."

"You know where she works?"

"No, but I can ask Kevin. He probably knows."

"You can if you want. It doesn't matter at this point. It's not like anyone has reported her missing."

"Other than Donny."

"He's an idiot."

I took a bite of my fish burger and washed it down with a gulp of Bud Light draft. "It's not my place to say, Rance, but I think Donny might be messing around with a married woman in the building."

"I didn't figure you as a gossip, Rex."

"That's not why I'm telling you. It's just that her husband is a pretty big guy and I don't want to see Donny get into any trouble."

"What's her name?"

"Frankie Salas."

"Tall, thin, redhead, fifty-something?"

"That's her."

"I know her. I'll talk to him about it."

"Anything else you want me to do about this Robin Day thing?"

"Just keep an eye out."

"For what?"

"I don't know. For anything."

"You got it."

I finished my burger and beer, and Rance finished his salad and water.

"It's only like one o'clock," I pointed out.

"Yeah, so?" Rance said.

"Aren't you going to be starving by two thirty?"

"I have a protein bar in my desk at the station."

"Yum," I said.

Chapter Five

Gayle had Thursday off as well, so she decided to ride over to Centre Street with me. She was going to do some shopping and then hang out at the book store with her friend Lori.

Lori Farber owned Island Books, right across the street from Collins' Hardware. Lori and her husband, Paul moved to Fernandina Beach from New York City several years ago and had been friends of ours almost since the day they got here.

All the way to work Gayle and I discussed Robin Day and her puppy. We also talked about Donny and his relationship with Frankie Salas.

"Come up with me," I said. "I'm going to check on the puppy and take it outside to go to the bathroom."

"You just want me to have a look around her apartment, don't you?" Gayle replied.

"That too," I admitted.

There were no parking spots, so I had to drive past the hardware store and Amelia Island Coffee.

"What's everybody looking at?" Gayle asked.

I glanced over on my way by to see Christine Collins, Janice Godfrey, Lloyd Cushing, and a few others standing in front of Collins' staring skyward. "I don't know," I said. I pulled into the first spot we came to and we got out.

"What's everyone looking at?" I asked, tilting my head upward. "Holy crap!" There was a girl standing on the ledge outside a window on the fourth floor.

"Get out of the way!" Gayle shouted. She ran through the front entrance to the apartment building and vaulted up the stairs.

I bolted around the corner of the building and ran down the hall to the elevator. I hit the button and the doors opened. I jumped inside and hit four over and over again. Then I hit the close door button. It seemed like it took forever to get to the fourth floor. The doors opened and I ran into the hall and toward the front of the building. Gayle was already standing at an open window.

"Come back inside, honey," Gayle said in a motherly tone that I wasn't used to hearing from her. "Come back in and we can talk about it."

The open window was the only window at the end of the hall; it overlooked Centre Street. The window's sill was level with the ledge. I cautiously moved closer to the window. It was wide enough that Gayle and I could both stick our heads through it. I inched closer and looked downward. It was a long way down. There were now about fifty people in the street and traffic had halted. I heard sirens off in the distance.

"I don't want to come back inside," the woman argued.

High Maintenance

I couldn't see her, but she sounded young, real young. I wanted to poke my head through the window, but didn't want to make things worse.

"What's your name?" Gayle asked.

"What do you care?" the girl hollered back

"Trust me, I care."

"You don't even know me. Why would you care?"

"You made me care," Gayle said, "when you decided to climb out on this goddamn ledge."

I tried to get a look, but all I could see was the toes of a pair of black Converse All-Stars sticking an inch over the ledge.

Gayle swung her leg up over the window ledge. I laughed nervously.

"Uh, honey, what are you doing?" I asked as calmly as I could. Gayle ignored me. I tried to pull her back inside. She shrugged me off.

"Don't!" said the girl. "I'll jump."

"I'm just going to sit out here on the ledge with you," Gayle said.

"Are you crazy?" I said.

"Yeah, lady, are you crazy?" the girl parroted.

Gayle's palms were on the ledge. She swung her other leg over the sill and inched her butt out onto the ledge. She was sitting with her legs dangling over the edge.

"Wow, this is kinda scary," said Gayle.

I knew Gayle was just making conversation, because I had never seen her scared of anything. Gayle was the toughest woman I ever met. Thinking back, the only time I ever saw her cry was when our son Ben drove away from the house pulling that U-Haul behind his Subaru, en route to college.

"My name's Gayle," she said.

"What are you even doing here?" the girl asked. "Do you live in this shitty building?"

Hey, I thought, *this building ain't shitty*. I looked back down the hall. *The hall could probably use a coat of paint. But shitty?*

"No," Gayle replied. "My husband is the maintenance man here."

"Sounds like a real loser."

Wow! Maybe I'll push her.

Gayle chuckled. "He's not a loser. He's retired."

"How old is the geezer?"

"He's forty-eight."

"And retired already? You guys loaded, or something?" she asked.

"No. We just played our cards right."

"What's that mean?"

"I was in the Navy for twenty years, and Rex had a successful construction company that he sold a few years ago."

"*Rex?*" she asked.

"That's my husband."

"Rex. Sounds like a dog's name."

I wish she had jumped before we got here.

"I wish my parents had played their cards right," said the girl.

There were three patrol cars out front of the hardware store now.

"What do your pare—"

"Stacy," the girl said. "My name is Stacy."

"What do your parents do, Stacy?" Gayle asked.

I looked over my shoulder to see two police officers coming down the hall toward me. I recognized them both. I put up my hand to slow them down. One of them nodded and they stopped.

"Do?" Stacy asked. "They don't *do* anything ... but he drinks, and they holler at each other, and my old man slaps my mom around ... when he's home, which is most of the time."

"I'm sorry about that, Stacy, but jumping off this ledge won't change them, it'll only change you. You'll be dead, and you'll never have a chance to play your own cards right."

Wow, that was good.

"Please, come back inside, and Rex and I will do anything we can to help you."

I leaned forward a little. I saw Stacy side-step toward Gayle. She reached out her hand and Gayle took it.

Stacy's foot slipped from the ledge and she stumbled toward Gayle. Gayle grabbed her with both hands. I threw my arms around Gayle's waist. Both officers ran to me, their hands grabbing whatever they could. The crowd below let out screams and shouts.

Gayle had a hold of Stacy's shirt in one hand and her forearm in the other.

"Help!" Stacy screamed.

"I got you!" Gayle shouted.

"I got you," I said.

One of the officers reached out the window and grabbed the waistband of Stacy's shorts and pulled.

Gayle pulled, and so did I. Gayle tumbled backwards through the window and onto the floor, with Stacy landing next to her. Everyone breathed a sigh of relief.

When we all got to our feet, one of the officers reached for Stacy. Gayle stepped in front of her.

"Don't touch her," Gayle warned.

"We have to take her in," one of them said.

"You'll have to go through me," Gayle said.

The officers looked at each other and then back at Gayle. They didn't know what to think.

"Listen guys," I said. I made eye contact with one of them. "Don't I know you? Bob, right? You live over behind my neighbor, Glenn Simon."

He nodded. "Yeah, on Lumina Court. Bob Whitmire."

"Bob, how about if you let my wife and I handle this. We'll give the girl a ride home—"

"I'm not going home," said Stacy.

Gayle shushed her.

"We'll give her a ride home," I continued. "We'll talk to her parents. You saw how good Gayle was out on that ledge. She knows what she's doing."

The officers looked at each other again.

"Fine with me," said Bob's partner. "Less paperwork for us."

"Yeah," Bob agreed, "as far as I'm concerned it was just some kid fartin' around."

High Maintenance

We shook hands and they left.

"Thanks for protecting me from those cops," Stacy said.

I turned around and looked at her. "I was protecting *them* from Gayle," I informed her. "I didn't want to see two cops' asses get kicked by a woman and then have them try to explain to everyone in town how it happened."

This was the first time I got a good look at Stacy. She couldn't have been more than fourteen years old. Her wide-set cornflower blue eyes sparkled with intelligence. There was a smattering of freckles around her slightly turned up nose. Her lips, shaped in a natural Cupid's bow, seemed to be always slightly parted, and her front teeth were large and prominent, with a small space between them. She had unnaturally black hair, undoubtedly dyed, with reddish-purple streaks. She was a few inches shorter than Gayle, and a little chunky. Not what anyone would call fat, just a little heavier than what most girls think they're supposed to be these days. I walked back down the hall toward the elevator and Gayle and her new friend followed.

We got on the elevator and I punched the two button.

"Where we going now?" Stacy asked.

"Rex wants me to look around an apartment for clues about a missing woman," Gayle answered.

Stacy perked up. "What are you, like a private dick or something?"

"No," said Gayle. "I'm a waitress."

"Private dick," I mumbled. "What is it, 1942?"

Once inside Robin Day's apartment, Stacy immediately spotted the dog. "A puppy!" she said, and spent the rest of her time in the apartment sitting on the couch petting the little guy. It's funny how someone letting you know they care about what happens to you—and the sight of a tiny puppy—can change a kid's entire outlook on things.

I filled the dog's water dish and food bowl. Stacy set him on the floor and he ran to the bowls. He was a lot more chipper than the day before.

Gayle walked into Robin's bedroom and returned a few minutes later with a small date book. She flipped through the pages. "It says here she has a hair appointment tomorrow morning at ten."

"Maybe she's coming back today," I offered.

Gayle picked up a framed five by seven photograph that was sitting on an end table. "You know this guy?" she asked. The photograph was a head-shot of Robin and a man posing cheek to cheek; they were both grinning big. There were pine-covered mountains in the background, so we knew the photograph wasn't taken in Florida.

"Maybe," I said. "She does have a boyfriend, I think. I've seen a guy here a couple times. That might be him."

Gayle took the picture out of the frame and put the frame back on the table. There was a time stamp in the lower right-hand corner of the photograph. Gayle read the date aloud. "July 7, 2017."

Gayle walked into the kitchen and stood in front of a calendar that hung on the wall near the fridge. Gayle and I had the same calendar. It was a Collins' Hardware calendar with a photograph of a local landmark on each month. This month was the Old Nassau County Courthouse. Gayle put her finger on one of the days. "Who's JB?" she asked.

"Jimmy Buffett?" I said.

Gayle shot me a look. "I doubt it. She wrote JB on almost every Tuesday and Friday for the last two months."

High Maintenance

"Maybe JB is her boyfriend," said Stacy. "Maybe he comes to see her every Tuesday and Friday."

"Yeah, maybe," I scoffed.

"You might be right," said Gayle.

Stacy gave me a snide little grin. "I might be right, *Rex*," she said.

Oh boy.

We looked around the apartment for another twenty minutes or so. Gayle wrote down some things on a piece of paper, like the name of Robin's hairdresser, and the initials JB. There was nothing in the apartment that we could find that told anything about Robin's past. Gayle thought if we knew where Robin worked, we could call and see if they said she was on vacation, but there was nothing in the apartment that even hinted at a job.

"Well, let's get out of here and lock up," I said.

"What about the puppy?" Stacy asked.

"He's staying here," I replied. My eyes strayed to the living room corner, where the dog had obviously done some more of his business. Stacy and Gayle followed my gaze; their noses wrinkled in distaste.

"The poor little dude can't stay here—it's cruel and unsanitary," said Stacey. She looked to Gayle. "He's probably lonely at night, all by his wittle self." She pouted her plump lips. That comment, delivered in baby-talk, reeled my tough-as-nails-but-with-a-heart-of-gold wife in like a trout.

"Let's bring him with us," said Gayle.

"Yeah," Stacy agreed, "let's bring him with us, Rex."

I knew when I was licked. I grabbed the dog food and dog dishes. Stacy grabbed the dog. Gayle grabbed a coat hanger out of Robin's closet and went out into the hall. I locked Robin's door. The three-I mean, four—of us trooped down the hall to the elevator.

"I hope you know what you're doing," I said, leaning in to Gayle's ear.

"Usually," Gayle replied.

We rode the elevator down to the ground floor and we walked around to the rear of the building. Robin's Kia was backed into one of the parking spots against the building. Gayle was able to unlock the door rather easily using the coat hanger. We searched the front and back seats, the glove box, and the trunk. Gayle even took a quick peek at the engine to make sure no one had tampered with it. I stood next to her as she inspected it. I stared at the engine too. I had no idea what I was looking for, since I didn't know the first thing about car engines ... or any other kind of engine, for that matter. Gayle slammed the hood and walked back around to the driver's side and got into the car. She put the seatbelt on.

"How tall is Robin?" Gayle asked.

"I don't know. Your height, probably. She's no taller than you."

Gayle stretched her legs to reach the gas pedal. She could reach it, but it didn't look comfortable for driving.

"What are you thinking?" I asked.

"The seat just seems a little too far back for someone my size."

"You think it means something?"

"It could mean something, it could mean nothing."

"I figured it was one of the two."

Stacy giggled.

Gayle got out of the car, hit the lock button, and shut the door. We walked back around the building to Centre

High Maintenance

Street. I reached into my pants pocket and pulled out my truck keys.

"Here," I said, handing them to Gayle. "You can take my truck home. I have some lights to install in the store."

"You want us to come back later and pick you up?" Gayle asked.

"No, that's okay. I don't know what time I'll be done. I'll find a ride home."

"Okay." Gayle kissed me good bye.

"Try to figure all this out before I get home."

"All what?"

Stacy was already to the truck, so I whispered, not wanting her to hear me. "The kid and dog situation," I said.

"Don't you worry about a thing," Gayle said, and gave me a sly little grin.

"I wasn't worried, but now I am."

Chapter Six

I worked a couple hours longer than usual to finish the new lighting in the basement over Kevin's workbench. I figured since I never went back and installed them the day before, like I said I would, I'd better finish them in one day. I also didn't want to get home too early, because I wanted to give Gayle plenty of time to get Stacy home and have a little talk with Stacy's parents. I was a little nervous about Gayle's interaction with the young girl's parents.

Gayle's mother passed away before I even met her, and she hasn't spoken to her father since she was eighteen years old. Nothing angered Gayle more than bad parents.

When I walked up out of the basement, Christine and Kevin were standing at the checkout counter. "All done?" Kevin asked.

"All done," I said. "You want to go down and take a look?"

"Nope."

"You want to give me a ride home?"

"What's the matter with your truck?"

"I sent Gayle home in it with that kid from this morning."

"What kid from this morning?"

Christine's eyes widened and she frantically shook her head no, trying to shut me up.

"Um," I said, "that kid from down the street."

"What kid?" Kevin asked again.

"You don't know her." I said.

"Then why did you bring it up"

"You asked about my truck."

Kevin was confused. "Whatever," he said. "Come on, I'll take you home."

I had worked for Kevin for over two years, and had been shopping in his store for the last twenty years, but this was the first time he had ever been to my house.

"Straight ahead," I said, pointing at my house, directly across from the entrance to the cul-de-sac.

Kevin pulled his Toyota Tacoma into my driveway, right next to my truck. He didn't shut off the engine, or even put it in park. I felt like I should ask him in for a beer. Maybe next time.

"Thanks for the ride," I said, and climbed out.

"Sure," he replied. "Anytime."

"Anytime?" I asked.

"Well, not anytime."

I chuckled and shut the door. The passenger side window was down, so I rested my forearms on the door. "Do you know where Robin Day works?" I asked.

"No," Kevin replied. "Why?"

"Rance asked me. Do you have a previous address on her?"

"I don't think so."

"Don't you make your tenants fill out a lease?"

"Yeah, but I don't ask a bunch of questions. The lease just says the rent is due every month on the first, and they have to give me a thirty-day notice if they're moving out."

"Alright," I said, and pushed myself away from the truck. "See you later."

Kevin backed out of the driveway and I went into the garage through the front screen door. Several years ago I had converted the garage into a family room. I built screen panels with a door that could be put up in the spring and taken down in the winter when we didn't use it as a family room.

The television was turned on in garage/family room, but no one was in there. I went through the door that lead to our living room. Oddly enough, the TV was on in there as well, but no one was watching it either. I hadn't seen two televisions on in the house with no one watching them since Ben moved out. I walked around the house and looked out into the backyard; nary a soul in sight. I returned to the driveway.

Chester Gable and his wife, Ho, were sitting in lawn chairs in *their* driveway. That's where you could find the Gables most evenings. The two sixty-somethings would come out in the afternoon around four, sit side by side in their lawn chairs, and have a couple beers. Between six and seven they would fold up the chairs and head back inside. Some nights Gayle and I would bring our lawn chairs over and join them. Sometimes Glenn Simon, my neighbor on the other side, would come over too. Glenn's wife, Daisy, rarely came over, unless she was looking for

Glenn. Glenn hadn't come over much in the last few weeks, because his doctor had told him to stop drinking alcohol.

"Hey, neighbor," Chester called out, holding his bottle of LandShark Lager in the air.

"Hey, Chester," I hollered back. "Evening, Ho."

Ho held up her bottle and grinned big.

"See ya got a new dog," Chester observed.

"Yeah," I replied. "For now, I guess."

"Cute little shit," Ho added.

I nodded. "He's a cutie, alright."

Just then I saw Gayle come around the corner off of Caprice Lane. She was walking the dog; Stacy walked along beside her.

As the two neared, and saw me standing in the driveway, they both gave a big wave over their heads. I returned a half wave.

I waited for them to arrive and said, "What's going on?"

Gayle knew I wasn't just making conversation. She knew I meant *why haven't you taken Stacy home?* I wondered if I was actually going to have to explain to Gayle that fourteen-year-old girls weren't like puppies. If you found an abandoned one, you didn't just get to bring it home and keep it.

Gayle and I had once talked about having another child—Gayle had always expressed her desire to have a daughter—but eventually decided against it. I hoped Gayle wasn't about to ask if she could keep Stacy if she promised to feed her, take care of her, and clean up after her.

"Just taking the dog for a walk," Gayle said matter-of-factly.

"I can see that," I responded.

Gayle wouldn't make eye contact with me.

"Stacy," I said. "Would you please take the dog out back and let him run around?"

"Sure, Rex," she replied happily. Stacy was a lot happier now than she was when she was standing on that ledge four stories above the pavement.

Gayle handed her the leash, and up the driveway she went.

"What's going on?" I asked again.

"Listen," Gayle said.

"Oh, I'm listening," I said.

"I took her home—"

"But you forget to leave her there."

"Will you let me finish?"

"Go ahead."

"So, I took her home."

"And?"

"Shush!"

"Sorry."

"When I got near Stacy's house she says, 'Pull over here and I'll walk the rest of the way.' I said, 'No, I'll take you to your door. I'd like to speak with your mom and dad.' She says, 'I don't think that's a very good idea.' Well, she was right, it wasn't a very good idea."

"What do you mean?"

"I told them what had happened with Stacy out on the ledge. I told them that I felt it was just a cry for help, and that I really didn't think she wanted to kill herself. I told them that I knew of a great therapist that Stacy could speak with. And I even offered to help them with the cost if it wasn't something they could afford right now."

"How did they feel about that?" I asked.

"Stacy's dad, George, told me to stick my opinions up my ass, and to get the hell out of their house. Then he grabbed me by the shoulder and tried to force me out."

"Tried to force you out?" I asked. "What did you do, Gayle?"

"It was awesome, Rex!" Stacy shouted from the screen door. I turned to see the smile on her face. She had been standing there the whole time with the dog in her arms. "Gayle knocked his arm away. Then she spun around and punched him in the head. Then she jumped up in the air and kicked him in the chest. It was so cool. I didn't even have time to blink. My old man flew backwards and landed right on his ass. He didn't know what hit him."

I glared at Gayle. "Awesome," I said. There was no excitement when I said it, only sarcasm and a little bit of anger.

Gayle shrugged. "He was drunk, Rex, and he put his hands on me first."

"In his own house," I argued. "You can be drunk in your own house, *and* you can kick people out of your own house if you want to."

"We'll agree to disagree on that," said Gayle.

I heard Stacy snicker behind me. "Agree to disagree," she repeated quietly.

"What about Stacy's mom?" I asked. "Now she's left there by herself to deal with him. Did you ever think about that?"

"Yes."

"And?"

"And Libby's lying down in the guest room."

"Libby?"

"That's Stacy's mom."

"In our guest room?"

"Yes."

"Oh my God!" I turned and stormed up the driveway. The smile had left Stacy's face. She had seen angry men before and didn't know what to expect. I pulled open the screen and stopped. "I'm not mad at you," I said.

Stacy smiled. "Thank you for letting us stay here," she said.

"You're welcome."

On my way across the family room, Stacy said, "Rex?"

I turned back. "Yeah?"

"Gayle said she would teach me to punch and kick, just like her."

"Swell," I said. "There's nothing better than a fourteen-year-old girl with fists of fury."

Chapter Seven

I don't work Fridays, and Gayle didn't have to be in until three, so I had her ride over to the hair salon with me. I didn't sleep very well the night before. I kept thinking about the cops showing up at our house in search of Stacy and her mom, or worse, Stacy's drunken dad showing up. Gayle slept like a log. We left the house at nine thirty; Stacy and her mother were still asleep.

Deena's Salon was housed in a one-story brick building on First Avenue. It was right next door to—and in the same building as—Island Vibe Surf Shop. The building sat right smack dab between Dairy Queen and Hammerhead's Beach Bar. When Gayle agreed to come with me, I knew I would be having lunch at Dairy Queen; Gayle was the biggest junk food junkie I had ever met.

I pulled into the parking lot and shut off the engine. We both got out of the truck and noticed right away that the place didn't open for another twenty minutes.

"I thought you said it opened at nine," I said.

"I thought it did," Gayle replied.

I leaned against the fender and folded my arms across my chest. "Now what do we do?"

"It's only twenty minutes. Calm down."

I made it about forty-five seconds before letting out a big sigh.

"Really?" Gayle asked. "Come on, let's go for a walk."

"Where?"

"On the beach."

We walked through the parking lot, across the street, and in between Hammer Head's and its two-tiered deck. We crossed A1A and went down the access path to the beach. Gayle kicked off her flip-flops and so did I. I held out my hand and Gayle took it. She kicked her flip-flops off to the side.

"You're just going to leave them there?" I asked.

"Yeah," she said.

"What if someone runs off with them?"

"Who would want an old pair of flip-flops?"

I kicked mine over near hers.

We walked along the beach watching the waves crash against the sand. It was a little windier than I liked, but it was better than being at work.

After we had walked past several beach houses, I said, "We should sell our house and move down here."

"We would both have to go back to work full-time to afford it," Gayle said.

"We'll stay where we are," I responded.

We walked for another ten minutes or so and I asked, "So, what are you going to do with all the new house guests?"

"I haven't decided," she replied. "What are your thoughts?"

"I have no thoughts on it. I'm leaving this whole thing up to you."

"Wise decision," said Gayle. After a contemplative pause she added. "Stacy's a great kid."

"She seems like a nice kid," I agreed.

"She's really smart, and very artistic."

"Artistic, how?"

"She draws and paints. She also writes poetry."

"That's cool."

"She gets picked on a lot at school."

"Artsy kids usually do."

"Libby says George has always been a pretty big drinker, but that things have gotten a lot worse since he lost his job. The more he drinks, the more violent he gets."

"That's too bad."

Gayle pulled out her cell phone and checked the time. "Might as well head back," she said.

We got back to the salon around nine-twenty and walked in. There was already an old lady sitting in one of the chairs.

"Excuse me," said Gayle.

The woman behind the counter looked up from her appointment book. "Yes?" she said.

"I'm Gayle Langley and this is my husband, Rex. We were wondering if we could ask you a few questions."

The thirty-something brunette looked a little nervous. "Is something wrong?"

"We're not sure," Gayle replied.

The woman glanced over at me, and then back at Gayle. "What is it?"

Gayle reached into the back pocket of her jean shorts and pulled out the photograph of Robin Day. Gayle had folded it in half and stuck it there before we left the house. Just the fact that Gayle folded it like that told me she didn't plan on returning it to Robin. I wondered if this was because her gut told her we weren't going to find the missing woman. I wanted to ask, but didn't know if I really wanted to hear the answer.

"Do you know this woman?" Gayle asked, holding up the photograph.

"Sure," the woman replied. "That's Robin. She's a regular here." She glanced down at the appointment book, and then up at the wall clock that hung over the door. "Robin has a hair and nail appointment at ten. She should be here any minute." The woman paused and studied our serious faces. "Hey, what's the deal? Did something happen to her?"

"We don't know," I said.

"One of her neighbors reported her missing a couple days ago," Gayle clarified. "We were just wondering if she had been in contact with you in the last few days. We knew she had a hair appointment, and wondered if maybe she canceled."

The woman looked back down at the appointment book. "She didn't cancel—I'd have made a notation if she had—and I haven't heard from her since she made the appointment, over a week ago."

"Do you know exactly what day she called to make the appointment?" Gayle asked.

"No, I don't write that down. I just remember it was at least a week ago." The woman scrunched up her face quizzically. "I'm a little uncomfortable giving out all this information," she said suspiciously. "You two cops?"

"We're working with Detective Calvin Rance on a civilian basis. You ever heard of him?" The hairdresser stared blankly at me. "We're good pals, Detective Rance and me," I added self-importantly.

"I was a military cop for twenty years; retired now," Gayle broke in. "Robin's a tenant in the building where my husband is a handyman." She made it sound like a venereal disease. "She hasn't been seen in a few days. Lots of folks are worried about her. Including us."

As usual, Gayle's candor brought out the best in people. The hairdresser smiled warmly and said, "What else you need to know?"

"Do you know anything about her personal life?" Gayle asked. "Like where she works, or has she ever mentioned a boyfriend?" Gayle held up the photograph again. "Do you know the gentleman in the photograph with her?"

The hairdresser shook her head. "He doesn't look familiar, and I don't ever remember her saying anything about a boyfriend."

"How about a place of employment?" I asked.

"No. Sorry."

"Can I give you my cell phone number?" Gayle requested. "If you think of anything, you can give me a call."

"Sure." The woman picked up a pen. Gayle rattled off her number and the woman jotted it down on a small notepad near the cash register.

"And your name is?" Gayle asked.

"Sherri," the woman replied. "Sherri James."

"Sherri, we're parked out front," Gayle said. "Would you mind if we sat out there and waited to see if Robin shows up?"

"No, that's fine. Sorry I couldn't be of more help."

"We appreciate your time, Sherri," Gayle said. "You have a good day now, hear?" We went out and got in the truck.

"Do you think she's going to show up?" I asked.

"No," Gayle replied. "But Dairy Queen doesn't open until eleven, so, we might as well cool our jets."

I turned my ignition back one click to the accessories position and tuned the radio to 96.9 The Eagle. The Who was singing "Behind Blue Eyes." I tapped the steering wheel to the beat and sang along.

"Who sings this?" Gayle asked.

"The Who," I replied.

"Right. Let's keep it that way," she said.

"Wow."

We sat there until eleven o'clock. By then it was obvious that Robin Day wasn't making it to her hair appointment.

"Shall we head over to Dairy Queen?" I asked.

"Let's go next door to the surf shop first," Gayle said. "I want to look at bathing suits, and I don't want to do it after I eat."

High Maintenance

I quickly agreed with that, remembering times in the past when we've gone somewhere to eat, and afterwards went to a clothing store. Somehow eating a small plate of food can turn a five-foot four inch, 128 pound woman into a giant fat lady who can't fit into anything in the store. The worst part is, I have to be the poor schlep standing there with an armful of clothing as Gayle walks in and out of the dressing room saying, "Look at me! I can't believe how fat I look in this. Do I look completely gross in this? Tell me the truth." The truth is, she looks great and doesn't look any different than she would have looked if she had tried the clothing on before she ate, but I can't say that, because then I'm a liar who won't tell her the truth.

We got back out of the truck and went into Island Vibe. Gayle spent forty minutes looking at and trying on bikinis. I wanted to look at surf boards and board shorts, but I wanted to see Gayle modeling bikinis even more. Evidently the sales kid wanted to watch that too, because he didn't stray too far from the changing room.

Gayle picked out two bikinis she wanted: a black one with a triangle top, and a halter top with red and white horizontal stripes. When we got to the checkout counter Gayle informed me that she hadn't brought any money. I gladly paid for the suits, and we left.

"Remind me and I'll pay you back when we get home," she said, on our way to Dairy Queen.

"Don't worry about it," I said. "I consider them a great investment—I'll get to enjoy them as much as you will, tits—er, toots."

"Aw, you're so sweet. Just for that I'll let you buy me lunch too."

"You treat me so well."

I ordered the Chicken Bacon Ranch sandwich with fries and a Coke. Gayle ordered the Kansas City BBQ

Pulled Pork sandwich on a pretzel roll. She had ordered that same thing the last three times we ate at Dairy Queen. She also got fries and a Coke.

I lingered around the condiment station while Gayle chose a table. When our order came up I brought it to the table and distributed our grub. Gayle always wanted to eat her food on the tray. After I sat down, I ogled her BBQ sandwich as she unwrapped it.

"You get that all the time. Must be pretty good," I remarked. "How 'bout letting me have a bite?"

Gayle pulled the tray toward her. "Get your own!" she growled with mock ferocity.

We were halfway through our meal when Gayle's cell phone rang.

"Hello?" Gayle answered. "When?" she asked. "We'll be right there." Gayle shoved the remaining half of her sandwich into her mouth. "Humompth!" She jumped up and headed for the door.

I figured "humompth" meant "Come on," so I ran to catch up with her.

I started the truck and backed out of the parking spot. What's the matter?" I asked.

"That was Stacy. She said her father is at the house."

"Our house?"

"Yes."

"Call the police," I said.

I drove as fast as I could and Gayle put in a call to 911. I drove down Taurus Court and straight across the cul-de-sac. I slammed on the brakes and skidded to a stop in our driveway. Stacy and her mom ran out to the truck.

"Where is he?" Gayle asked.

"He left," Stacy said.

Gayle looked at Libby. "Are you okay?"

Libby nodded her head. "Yes, I'm fine. Just a little shaken up."

I walked up the driveway toward my broken screen door. One of the 3x7 screen panels was also smashed. "Dammit," I said quietly.

A cop car pulled up behind my truck, his light bar was flashing but his siren was off.

"Where's the dog?" Gayle asked.

"He's in the house," Libby replied.

"Everyone okay?" asked the officer. It was Bob Whitmire.

"My screen seems to be the only casualty, Bob," I said.

"What happened?"

We explained the entire situation to Bob and I told him I did want to press charges. Libby gave Bob her address so he could go arrest her husband. We thanked him and he left.

"Let's get you two inside," Gayle said. "Have you eaten?"

"No," Stacy replied.

"I'll make you something."

Sleeping in my beds, breaking my house, eating my food, I thought. *This just keeps getting better and better.*

Chapter Eight

Officer Whitmire contacted me on Saturday afternoon to let me know that George Dawes had been arrested and charged with menacing and destruction of private property. He was given an appearance ticket and released under his own recognizance. I put Libby on the phone, and Whitmire asked her if she wanted to come down and fill out an order of protection; she declined the offer. Gayle urged Libby to change her mind, but Libby said that George being arrested the night before was probably enough to straighten him out. Libby reasoned that she and Stacy would have to return home sooner or later, and that maybe it wasn't such a good idea to push things. Unbeknownst to Gayle and me, Libby had spoken by phone with George earlier in the day, and George had apologized for everything, and pleaded for her return.

Gayle and I stood in the doorway of the guest bedroom as Libby put the clothes she had brought with her into a small backpack. "You can stay a few more days, if you want to," Gayle said.

"I appreciate that, and am thankful for everything you've done," Libby replied. "But Stacy and I should really get home. Poor George isn't very good at taking care of himself."

"Yeah," I mumbled. "Poor George."

"Can Stacy stay a few more days, at least?" Gayle asked. "Maybe you and George need some time alone."

Libby looked up from her bag and smiled. "If she wants to, she can."

In the driveway, Stacy hugged her mom goodbye. Libby and I climbed into my truck, and I drove her home. Libby was quiet the entire trip. I stole several glances at her. Libby had the same sad, cornflower blue eyes and upturned nose as her daughter, but the resemblance ended there. Libby was thin and haggard—somewhat "hard looking," as my dad used to say about women who'd been knocked around physically and emotionally. She had one of those faces you knew were pretty once, and maybe could be again, under different circumstances. For her sake, I hoped so.

When we got to her house, I walked Libby to the door. George greeted us with a smile. He shook my hand and said he was sorry for what had happened. He offered to repair any damages to our house. I told him that wouldn't be necessary.

"Where's Stacy?" George asked.

"She's going to stay with the Langleys for a few more days," Libby replied.

"That's good," said George. "Maybe we could use some time alone." He hugged his wife and kissed her on top of the head.

I turned and walked back out to my truck.

High Maintenance

When I returned home, and walked through the broken screen door, Stacy was sitting on the couch in the family room watching TV. The puppy was lying beside her. "How did it go?" she asked, without taking her eyes from the screen. She was flipping through the channels without staying on any one long enough to see if there was anything worth watching. I hated when people did that.

"Good," I replied.

"Did he tell you both how sorry he was?"

"Yup."

"He's good at that."

"Maybe things will get better."

"Maybe."

I knew things weren't going to get better, and so did Stacy. But I was glad she was here and not there.

"Where's Gayle?" I asked.

"She said she was going to look for something for dinner."

"She won't find anything," I said. "We'll be going out to dinner." I sat down in my recliner. "What are you watching?"

Stacy pointed the remote at the TV and turned the channel to the Ray's game. "I was just watching the Rays/Yankees game," she said.

Good girl, I thought. "You like the Rays?" I asked.

"No," she replied. "I like the Yankees."

Bad girl. Bad girl.

Chapter Nine

Gayle worked Saturday evening, and most of Sunday, so I was stuck at home entertaining a fourteen-year-old girl. We watched baseball together both days, and took the dog for walks a bunch of times. I introduced Stacy to Chester and Ho Gable, and to Glenn and Daisy Simon. Stacy's mom called her a few times to see how she was doing, and told her that George hadn't had a drink since Friday. I have to admit, I was a little surprised by that. Stacy spent a lot of time drawing in her sketch pad with colored pencils. Gayle was right, she was really good. She did a sketch of me as I watched TV, and she did one of the dog lying on the couch. I complimented Stacy, but told her she'd failed to capture my basic rugged manliness. Without missing a beat, she said, "God did, too." I was beginning to like this quick-witted kid—smart mouth and all.

Monday morning Gayle and I dropped Stacy off at Fernandina Beach Middle School. Stacy had expressed her hatred of school several times, but we let her know that if she was staying with us, going to school was a necessity. She reluctantly agreed to go.

We sat in the parking lot and watched to make sure Stacy actually went inside. When she got to the door, she turned, flashed us a smile, and waved. Gayle waved back, and we drove away.

I pulled the truck into a parking spot in front of the Pineapple Patch clothing store and we got out. As we walked past Amelia Island Coffee we waved at Janice through the window, and she waved back. We went around the side of the hardware store, through the door, and down the hall to the elevator.

"You think Rance will do this?" I asked.

"I would think so," Gayle replied. "It's been several days now and still no sign of Robin. We'll also inform him that she didn't show up for her hair appointment Saturday morning."

We rode the elevator up to the second floor and went to Robin's door. I unlocked it and we went inside.

In the kitchen sink there was a coffee mug and a drinking glass. Gayle picked up the drinking glass with her fingertips. "Look for a Ziploc bag or something to put this in," she said.

I opened and shut drawers until I found a box of freezer bags. "This good?" I asked.

"Perfect," Gayle replied.

I handed her the bag and she gently slipped the glass inside and zipped it shut.

"Let's go," she said. "I need a cup of coffee."

We stopped at Amelia Island Coffee and grabbed three coffees to go. One for me, one for Gayle, and one for Detective Rance. Gayle said it was always a good idea to bring a cop a cup of coffee, and even a donut, when you were about to ask them to do something for you. I told Gayle we better just stick to coffee, because Rance was some kind of a health nut, and until they started making a donut salad with a side of fat-free dressing, he wouldn't be interested.

On our way to the police station, Gayle got on her cell phone and made a call to a friend of hers, Larry Stoner with a regional office of the Florida Department of Law Enforcement, owed her a favor.

"Larry, you fat old piece of shit!" Gayle hollered into her phone.

What a lady, I thought.

"It's Gayle. Yeah, yeah, you limp-dick douche. I toldja never to bring that up." She shot me a mysterious smile and continued.

"Hey, Larry, the reason I'm calling is, I need a favor. Yeah, today. Like in a few hours."

Gayle and her buddy Larry spoke for another few minutes. She called him a few more names, some I didn't think people were supposed to use anymore in this politically correct society. I couldn't hear everything Larry was saying, but I think I should have been angry at what I did hear. I know people use the excuse "boys will be boys," but it's a little weird when one of the boys is your wife.

We arrived at the police station, and I approached the female cop at the front desk. "Hey, is Detective Rance around?"

She came back with, "Can I ask what this is about?"

"I'm a friend of his. I told him I was stopping by and he asked me to bring him a coffee."

The woman looked puzzled. "Coffee?" she asked.

"It's decaf." *Quick thinking.*

She smiled, nodded, and pressed a button on the intercom. "Rance, your buddy is here with the coffee you ordered." She looked back up at me. "He'll be right out."

We waited a few minutes and Rance stuck his head through a door to our right. "Oh, it's you."

I held up the coffee. "Got your coffee."

"Is it decaf?"

"Yup."

"Thanks." Rance took the coffee and pulled off the lid. He took a deep breath, breathing in the coffee's aroma. "Where'd this come from?"

"Amelia Island Coffee," said Gayle.

Rance took a sip and nodded his approval. "What can I do for you two?" he asked.

Gayle held up the clear freezer bag. "Robin Day still hasn't turned up," she explained. "It's been a week since your nephew reported her missing."

"Has it been a week already?" Rance asked.

"It'll be a week tomorrow," I responded.

"Rex and I went to her hair salon Saturday morning where she was supposed to show up for an appointment she had scheduled for ten o'clock. She didn't show, nor did she cancel that appointment."

"What's the glass?" Rance asked.

"We pulled it out of her kitchen sink," Gayle said. "We were hoping her fingerprints were on it and we could get a match."

"We?" Rance asked.

"You," Gayle said.

"It's going to take a week or so to get those results back," Rance said.

"I spoke to a friend of mine at the FDLE," Gayle said. "If Rex and I run the sample down to him, he said he'll do it this afternoon."

"Oh he did, did he?"

"Yeah, we just need you to fill out the form and sign it."

Rance took another sip of his coffee, breathed in, and sighed. "Fine," he said. "But this better not come back on me in any way, shape, or form."

Gayle and I thanked him, jumped in my truck, and headed for Jacksonville. Rance assured us he would make out the necessary paperwork and email it to Larry.

"That wasn't decaf," Gayle said, when we left the building.

"I know," I replied. "I figured the caffeine would motivate him."

Chapter Ten

After dropping the drinking glass off with Larry Stoner at the FDLE regional office, we took A1A home and stopped at Bob's Steak and Chop House for a late lunch. We made it back to Fernandina Beach just in time to pick up Stacy from school.

"How was your day?" Gayle asked.

"Good," Stacy replied.

"Learn anything new?" I asked.

Gayle looked at me and smiled. She remembered I used to ask Ben the same thing every day when he got home from school.

"No," said Stacy.

"Nothing?" I asked.

Stacy stared out the truck window as we drove along. "Well, I learned that Vincent Van Gogh only sold one painting in his whole life. He hardly ever worked at a real job, and his brother usually had to support him."

"What was his brother's name?" Gayle asked.

"Theo," Stacy replied.

"Where did he live?" Gayle asked.

"A lot of places, but he was born in Holland. He painted *The Starry Night* and *Irises* while he was in a nuthouse."

"When did he die?" I asked.

"I can't remember the date, but he shot himself when he was thirty-seven."

"Sounds like you learned something," I said.

"Shut up," she grumbled.

"I know," I said. "It sucks to learn stuff."

Stacy didn't look over, but I could tell she was grinning.

"Do you need anything while we're out?" Gayle asked.

"I could use some more of my clothes," Stacy said.

"You want me to drive by your house?" I asked.

"I don't want to go there," Stacy replied.

"How about if we drop you off at our house, and then Rex and I run over there and pick some stuff up for you?"

"That would be good," said Stacy.

We pulled into the driveway and I walked Stacy to the door. "Make sure you take the dog out first thing," I said.

"I will," she replied.

"You're probably going to have to come up with a name for that thing."

"Won't that confuse him?"

High Maintenance

"What do you mean?"

"When his owner comes home, she'll start calling him by his old name."

"We'll cross that bridge when we come to it," I said, knowing we may never come to it.

"Okay," Stacy said, and went inside.

When I got back to the truck, Gayle was on her cell phone. "Okay," she said. "Whatever you have to do. Thanks, Larry. Talk to you later."

"What's up?" I asked.

"Larry says they're having trouble pulling a fingerprint off the glass, they're going to try Super Glue fuming this afternoon when the chamber is free."

"Super Glue fuming?" I asked. "What's that?"

"They put the glass in what's called a Super Glue chamber," Gayle explained. "It basically looks like a large glass cabinet. Then they put some Super Glue in the chamber with the glass, and heat it up. The glue will then stick to the fingerprint. It becomes more pronounced, and easier to lift."

"Huh. That's cool." I started the truck and backed out of the driveway.

"I also asked Larry to give us a call before he sent his findings to Rance."

"Sneaky."

"It's in my nature."

"Hey, can you give Ho a call and let her know that Stacy's at the house alone? I told her to take the dog out."

"Sure," Gayle said, and reached for her cell phone.

We pulled to the curb in front of George and Libby's place a few minutes later and got out.

"The car isn't here," Gayle noticed. "I wonder if they're not home."

"We'll know soon enough," I replied.

Gayle walked up the concrete walkway just like a cop. Her eyes darted from door to window to window, and to the nearby houses. She was always alert, and ready for whatever might happen. She always impressed me.

I knocked on the front door, and a minute later Libby answered. She smiled, and then looked concerned. "Where's Stacy?" she asked, looking past us. "Is everything okay?"

"Everything's fine," Gayle assured her. "Stacy's at our house. We just stopped by to pick up a few of her clothes."

Libby put her hand on her chest. "Oh, thank goodness. Silly me, I'm always expecting the worst. Come in."

Gayle and I walked into the living room. "Is everything okay here?" I asked.

"Yes, everything is good," Libby responded.

"Where's George?" Gayle asked.

"He's at work."

"Work?" Gayle asked, probably sounding a little bit too surprised.

"He went back to work this morning. A friend of his called him last night and said they needed someone over at Dunham Lumber Yard in Jacksonville, but that he had to start this morning. George jumped at the chance."

"That's great," I said.

"Yeah, great," said Gayle, with a lot less enthusiasm than me. "Is it full time?"

High Maintenance

"Forty hours a week," Libby answered. "And it's two dollars an hour more than he was making at Elliott's Lumber."

Libby was proud of her husband, but that didn't change the way Gayle felt about him. Gayle had spent too many of her childhood years watching her own father turn over a new leaf, and then watch him slap the shit out of her mother a week later. As far as Gayle was concerned, people didn't change.

Gayle followed Libby into Stacy's bedroom, and I waited in the living room. Ten minutes later they returned, Gayle holding a small pink duffel bag in one hand and a pair of black sneakers in the other,

"I spoke with Stacy again last night," said Libby. "I told her about her dad's new job. I'm surprised she didn't mention it."

"It probably just slipped her mind," I said.

"Probably," Gayle agreed.

"I told her she could come home any time she liked," said Libby. "She said maybe the end of the week. Would that be okay?"

"Libby, Stacy can stay with us as long as she likes," Gayle said. "And you can come back any time you like as well."

"Thank you so much," said Libby. She and Gayle hugged goodbye.

On the way home I said to Gayle, "That's awesome that George got a new job."

"Ya think?" was Gayle's reply.

"Stacy said her mom told her George had quit drinking too," I threw in.

"Most people don't quit, Rex, they just stop for a while."

"Maybe George isn't most people."

"Thank God for that."

Chapter Eleven

Larry Stoner called the next morning, about a half hour after we dropped Stacy off at school. Gayle put it on speaker. He told Gayle that there was a thumbprint that didn't get a match, but that one of the fingerprints did. The print belonged to a man by the name of Trenton Boyd. Trenton Boyd had been arrested in Orlando in 2003 for stealing a car with some friends and taking it for a joyride. From what Larry could see, Trenton had stayed out of trouble since then.

"What's his last known address?" Gayle asked.

"2413 Lake Sunset Drive in Orlando," said Larry. "But like I said, that was fifteen years ago."

"You have a phone number?"

"Sure," Larry said, and rattled it off.

"Thanks, Larry," Gayle said. "Can you email me everything you have there? And while you're at it, see if you can go ahead and forget to send it to Fernandina PD."

"You got it, Stump Grinder," said Larry.

Gayle shot me a look out of the corner of her eye and her face reddened a little. "Thanks, Larry," she said again, and hung up.

"Stump Grinder?" I asked.

"It's a long story," Gayle replied.

"I don't even want to know."

"It was an undercover thing and—"

"Really, I don't want to know."

Gayle started dialing her cell. "I'm going to go ahead and call this number now." She put it on speaker again.

An elderly woman answered. "Hello?" she said.

"Good morning, ma'am," said Gayle. "This is Detective Monica Geller with the Miami-Dade Sheriff's Department. I'm following up on a hit-and-run that occurred last week. Can I please speak with Trenton Boyd?"

"Oh, my," said the woman. "Was Trenton injured?"

"No, ma'am. A car ran into Mr. Boyd's car and then left the scene. We've identified the driver of the vehicle, and I just wanted to touch base with Mr. Boyd."

"Well, he doesn't live here anymore. I'm his mother."

"Oh, okay. This address was listed on my database. Do you have his current address and phone number?"

"Yes, I do." The woman gave Gayle Boyd's number and then excused herself to retrieve her address book. Mrs. Boyd returned to the phone and said, "Trent's address is 8 Dallyon Avenue, St. Augustine, Florida, 32080."

"Is he still employed with Nationwide?" I knew Gayle was just throwing a name out there.

"Nationwide?" Mrs. Boyd asked. "No, he works at Bank of America. He's been the manager there for five years."

"The Bank of America on Elm Street?" Gayle fished.

"The one across from the college."

"Thank you very much, Mrs. Boyd."

"Do you know if it was Trent or his wife who was driving the car at the time?" Mrs. Boyd asked.

Gayle and I looked at each other. "It was Trent, ma'am," Gayle confirmed.

"Oh, that's good."

Gayle hung up, and went into the guest room to check her email.

I followed her in. "That was pretty good," I said.

"Don't be too impressed," she said. "That shit only works on old people."

Gayle opened the email from Larry and printed off Boyd's arrest record, his photograph, and the fingerprint report.

"How long you known Larry?" I asked.

"Since I was stationed in San Diego," Gayle replied. "Holy shit."

"What?"

"It's the guy in the photograph from Robin's apartment."

"And according to the time stamp on that picture," I said, "if he's been married for more than a year, then he's been a naughty boy."

"Yup."

"What's next?" I asked.

"We give Trenton Boyd a call."

"Now?"

"Nope. When we get to St. Augustine."

"We're going to St. Augustine?"

"Yup."

"I thought you had to work this afternoon."

"I'm calling in sick. This is way more fun than waiting tables."

Chapter Twelve

On our way to St. Augustine, Gayle did an internet search for Bank of America; there were four of them in the St. Augustine area. The one at the corner of Cathedral Place and Cordova Street was right across the street from Flagler College, so we figured that was the one. We reached the bank at eleven forty-five and parked on Cathedral Place. Gayle took out her phone and dialed the number Boyd's mother had given us.

"Hello?" a man said.

"Is this Trenton Boyd?" Gayle asked.

"May I ask who is calling?"

"You can ask."

"Who is this?"

"Trent, we'd like to speak to you about Robin Day."

There was a long pause. Gayle didn't speak either. I figured she was letting a few scenarios play out in Boyd's head.

Finally he said, "Robin who?"

That made Gayle chuckle. "Good one, Boyd," she said. "We're sitting out front of your bank right now and we're starving. How about if you take us to lunch, and we'll get to the bottom of this?"

"I could call the cops."

"We could go ask your wife the questions instead."

"Where are you parked?"

"On Cathedral. We're in a red and white Ford F-150."

"Give me ten minutes."

"I'm really hungry. If you're not out here in five, we go see what your wife is serving for lunch."

Boyd was standing at my truck window within five minutes. Nothing speeds up a guy like threatening to tell his wife about his extramarital dick swinging. He didn't look as happy as he did in the photograph with Robin Day. Boyd looked to be in his early thirties. He was average height, had nice teeth that were obviously professionally whitened. His hair was shaved down to about four days growth, and you could see where the bald spots would be if he let it grow out. He wore a light gray suit and a black tie.

"What is it you want?" Boyd demanded.

"We just want to ask you a few questions," I said.

Boyd pointed behind him. "My car's in the parking lot. You can follow me."

We watched Boyd climb into an emerald green late model Jaguar F-type coupe. The V8 roared like some mythological beast as he zoomed out of the parking lot.

"I hope he doesn't make a run for it," I commented. "Don't think I'll catch him."

High Maintenance

"We know where he lives," said Gayle.

Boyd took a right onto Cordova and drove about four blocks before pulling into a public parking lot; I pulled in beside him. I started for the pay station and Boyd said, "Don't worry about it. I know the guy."

I looked toward the attendant's shack. A big, muscular man with no neck wearing navy track pants and a red sleeveless T-shirt was watching us. Boyd waved, and the guy waved back. The three of us crossed the street to a place called Scarlett O'Hara's.

Scarlett O'Hara's was a pub that looked like an old rustic bungalow. The clapboards and trim were unfinished wood. A white picket fence separated the side of the building from the sidewalk on Cordova Street. We walked up the front steps from Hypolita Street and onto a porch that spanned the entire front of the building. Boyd pulled open the door and stepped back for Gayle and me to enter.

The interior was dimly lit with amber lighting. Everything was wood. The floors were oak planks, the bar was pine and varnished with a high-gloss urethane. Most of the walls were pine with a few sections of exposed brick here and there.

Except for a portrait (in an unbelievable tacky gilded frame) of Vivian Leigh as the beauteous and willful Southern belle in *Gone With the Wind*, I saw nothing to indicate how the pub got its name. A quick glance at a brochure I picked up at the hostess podium, however, revealed that the establishment had been created by combining two 1879 homes, and was reputed to be haunted. Well, fiddle-de-dee!

Boyd pointed to an empty four top across the room and we sat. A waitress came over and took a drink order.

"I have to use the restroom," Boyd said. "When I get back I want to know what this is all about."

The waitress brought our drinks, and ten minutes later I went looking for Boyd. He wasn't in the men's room, or the women's room. I walked to a side entrance and looked out to an outdoor bar that sat underneath a tin roof. Boyd wasn't there either.

"He split," I told Gayle, when I got back to the table.

"Are you shittin' me?" she asked. "I did not see that coming."

I tossed a twenty onto the table and we left.

"What an idiot," Gayle said, on our way down the front steps. "He's knows we're just going to go see his wife now."

When we got to the corner, Boyd was on his way back across the street toward us. Walking with him was the parking attendant and another smaller, younger man.

"Look at this freak show," Gayle said.

The parking attendant cracked his knuckles as he approached.

Gayle cracked her knuckles as well. She was doing it to poke fun at the muscle head. I stepped in front of her and put out my hands. They weren't stopping. "Listen guys—" That's when Muscles hit me in the gut. It felt like every bit of air that was inside me escaped. I tried to take a few steps back, but I tripped over my own feet and hit the cement hard on my ass.

Gayle spun toward me and the other guy threw his arms around her and spun her back. Boyd hit Gayle in the face with a right and then a left.

Muscles bent down and grabbed the front of my shirt. I brought up my foot, kicking him in the balls. A kick to the balls was my best move—that, and pulling hair. I did not possess the skills of my wife. She always said she could teach me a few things, but I felt stupid having my wife teach me how to fight. At times like these, however, I wished I had put my pride aside and let her school me.

Muscles grabbed his crotch and fell to his knees. I jumped to my feet and kicked him in the chin as hard as I could.

Gayle brought up her feet and kicked Boyd in the chest, sending him stumbling backwards. Then she snapped her head back, smashing her skull into her restrainer's nose. He quickly let go of her and grabbed his face.

Gayle turned, ripped a picket from the fence, and swung it with all her might, hitting Muscles in the back of the head. He fell face first into the sidewalk. She then turned her attention back to her opponent. She swung the picket again, smacking him in the side of the head.

Gayle didn't realize when she swung the picket that there was a four-penny nail still sticking through it. The small nail was embedded in the man's head, and the picket stayed there. Gayle snickered at the sight of the dangling picket.

Boyd turned and started running back toward the parking lot. I took off after him and caught him at his car. I grabbed him by his shirt with both hands and shoved him against the Jag. "That was really stupid, Boyd." I let go of him with my right hand and hit him as hard as I could. "*Really* stupid," I repeated.

I looked back toward Scarlett O'Hara's. Gayle was crossing the street and coming my way. Muscles was still face down, and the other guy was trying his best to remove the ring-shank nail from his head.

I hit Boyd again just for fun. I figured Gayle was probably going to hit him again too. I was right. She hit him about five times before he cried out, "Stop! Please!"

"And that's why you never hit a woman, Boyd," I told him.

He was on all fours, sobbing.

"Are you crying, you little bitch?" Gayle asked. She slapped him on the side of the head for good measure.

"Now tell us what you know about Robin Day," Gayle ordered.

"Okay! Okay!" Boyd shouted.

I helped him to his feet. Gayle stepped back; she was readying herself to strike again.

"Where's Robin?" I asked.

I glanced back at Gayle. She was inspecting her bruised and bloody knuckles.

"I don't know," Boyd said.

Gayle stutter-stepped and put up her fist.

Boyd flinched and put up his hand for protection. "Really!" he said. "I haven't seen her in two weeks."

"Then why all these theatrics?" Gayle demanded, waving her hand back toward Boyd's buddies.

"I just wanted them to scare you away. I didn't want you saying anything to my wife. I thought you were the ones trying to blackmail me."

"Blackmail you?" I said. "What are you talking about?"

"Someone contacted me about two weeks ago," Boyd explained. "They said if I didn't pay them, they were going to tell my wife."

"How much money did they ask for?" Gayle asked.

High Maintenance

"They told me they would call back with an amount and where to meet, but they never called back. That was two weeks ago."

"And you thought we were them," I said.

"Well, yeah. What would you think?"

"I would have thought first," I answered. "And not gotten myself into a mess like this."

I kept checking with Boyd's friends. They had gotten to their feet and were headed our way.

"Tell your friends to keep moving," I said. "You don't want to make Gayle angry. You wouldn't like her when she's angry."

Boyd waved them off and they kept walking. I watched out of the corner of my eye until they disappeared into the attendant's shack.

"Why haven't you been to see her in the last two weeks?" Gayle asked.

"I ended it with her the day after I got the call."

"How long were the two of you together?" Gayle asked.

"About a year and a half."

"And your wife never suspected?" I asked.

"No," Boyd replied. He gave us a look like we must be stupid, thinking he could possibly get caught. "We were careful."

"Oh," Gayle said, and gave me a look. "They were careful."

"You had no idea she was missing?" I said.

"How would I have known? I told her I couldn't see her anymore and asked her not to call me. I just assumed she was respecting my wishes."

"Where does Robin work?" asked Gayle.

"She works at an insurance company in Jacksonville."

"Which one?" Gayle asked.

"An Allstate office on Dunn Avenue. Her boss is Paul Clapp. Maybe he can tell you something."

We'll look into it," said Gayle. "Has she had any problems in the past with her boss, or any coworkers?"

"Not that I know of."

"Has she ever mentioned anyone with the initials JB?" Gayle asked.

Boyd thought for a second, and whispered "JB" a couple times. "Not that I recall," he said.

"Do you know anything about her parents?" I asked.

"Not really, they both passed away when she was young."

"Where was she from?" Gayle asked.

"Upstate New York. A town in the Adirondacks."

"The photograph of you and Robin that sits on her end table, is that where that picture was taken?" Gayle asked.

"Yes, it was taken near where she grew up. We spent the weekend there."

"Where did your wife think you were at the time?" I asked.

"A banking conference."

"Does Robin have any other family that you know of?" Gayle asked.

"No. She was an only child, and she never mentioned any aunts or uncles or any other relatives. Wait, she did say once that her mother's parents were still alive, but I don't know anything about them or where they live."

Gayle backed up a couple steps. "We have your cell phone number and your home address, Boyd. We also know where you work. I hope there's not going to be any reason for us to come back down here."

"There won't be," Boyd assured us.

"You know," I put in, "if for some reason the police decide to get involved, your wife will probably be questioned about this."

Boyd shook his head. "Yeah, I figured that much."

"You might want to think about preparing her for it."

"Is there anything else you can think of that might help our investigation?" Gayle asked.

Our investigation, I thought. *That's cool.*

Boyd shook his head. "No, but … can you let me know when you find her?"

"No," Gayle replied. She turned and opened the passenger side door of my truck. She took a piece of paper and a pen out of her pocketbook and wrote down her cell phone number for Boyd. "Here. If you think of anything else, give me a call."

As we pulled out of the parking lot and drove up Cordova Street, Gayle turned to me. "You wouldn't like her when she's angry?"

"That was the first thing that came to my mind."

"I'm not the Incredible Hulk you know."

"Well … you're not green, but—"

"But, what?"

"You kinda tear shit up when you get angry."

"I saw you kicking and punching too."

"Yeah, but I was just defending myself. I wasn't enjoying it like you were."

"Enjoying it?"

"Gayle, you laughed when that picket got stuck to the side of that guy's head."

Gayle busted out laughing. "You gotta admit, Rex, that was pretty funny."

I grinned. "Yeah, I guess."

"Some wives enjoy baking muffins. I, on the other hand, enjoy kicking the shit out of assbags."

"Your muffins are pretty good too."

"Now I'm in the mood for muffins."

Chapter Thirteen

When we arrived at home, Chester and Ho were sitting in their lawn chairs enjoying a cold beverage. Stacy was sitting Indian-style in the grass next to the driveway. Her sketchpad was in her lap, and a can of Diet Coke sat next to her. Stacy looked up and grinned big when she saw us pull into our driveway.

"How did everything go?" I asked, as I walked up Chester's walkway.

"Like clockwork," Chester replied.

"What the hell happened to you?" Chester gasped.

Stacy looked up from her sketchpad. "Oh my God!"

Ho was out of her chair and moving toward Gayle.

"It's nothing," Gayle said, gently poking the purple welt under her right eye. "It doesn't even hurt."

"You should see the other guy," I commented, trying to make light of the situation.

Chester looked back to me. "How come you don't have a mark on you?"

"I got hit in the stomach," I replied.

"Mm-hmm," said Chester.

"Gayle, tell him."

Ho was inspecting the lump on Gayle's cheek and the cut over her left eye. "Honey, you should let me put something on that."

"It's fine, Ho," Gayle said. "It's not the first time I've been hit, and it probably won't be the last." She glanced down at Stacy. "Homework?" she asked.

"Already finished it," Stacy replied.

"We took the dog for a walk," said Ho, still looking Gayle over. She took Gayle's hands and looked at her bruised knuckles. Ho just shook her head.

"I named him Vincent," said Stacy.

"Vincent?" Gayle asked.

"After Vincent Van Gogh," Stacy said.

"If that damn dog cuts off his own ear," Chester said, "don't come cryin' to me."

"Actually," Stacy said, "some scholars believe that Van Gogh actually lost his ear in a sword fight."

Chester climbed out of his chair with a groan. "Well, this scholar believes he needs another beer. You want one, Rex?"

"Sure, Chester," I replied.

"Gayle?"

"No, thanks. I'm good."

Ho shook her almost empty bottle in the air. "I'm ready."

High Maintenance

Chester walked into the garage and returned seconds later holding two Land Sharks. He handed one to me and I twisted off the top.

"You hungry?" Gayle asked.

"I'm starving," Stacy replied.

"Me too," I said. "We never got any lunch today."

"Rex is going to run to the grocery store and grab something to put on the grill," Gayle said.

"I am?" I asked.

"You and Chester come over too," Gayle said.

"We don't want to be a bother," said Ho.

"Speak for yourself," Chester said. He handed Ho her beer.

"Come over for dinner and I'll let you put a couple Band-Aids on me," Gayle offered.

"You got a deal," Ho replied.

Gayle and I turned and started down the driveway. "You coming, Stacy?" Gayle asked.

"Let me just finish this sketch and then I'll be home."

That was the first time Stacy called our house "home." I caught it, and I was sure Gayle did too, but I didn't say anything.

Gayle walked me to my truck and I got in. "When are we going to talk with Robin's boss?" I asked.

"I have to work tomorrow," Gayle said. "I can't call in again."

"Thursday morning?" I suggested.

"Sounds good," Gayle said, and pushed my door closed.

101

"You think there's any chance she's alive?" I asked.

"No," Gayle said. "Not after two weeks. At this point I just want to know what happened."

"Me too," I said.

Chapter Fourteen

Gayle received a phone call from Larry Stoner on Wednesday afternoon. He told her that Detective Rance had called him inquiring about the fingerprint results from the drinking glass. Larry fibbed a little, telling Rance that he hadn't gotten the results back yet, but expected them later in the day, and would send them out first thing Thursday morning.

After dropping Stacy off at school on Thursday, we headed for Jacksonville. On the way, I commented that, besides the fact that a young girl was missing, I was having a lot of fun with this investigation, and that it was a lot like being a private investigator. Gayle shot me a look and quickly reminded me that private investigators get paid, and that we were just a couple of people sticking our nose in other people's business.

We arrived at the Allstate office on Dunn Avenue a little before nine thirty. I pulled my truck into the driveway, and we went inside.

A gray-haired woman in her mid-sixties greeted us from behind a desk. "Good mawnin'," she said with a great big Allstate smile. "What can I do for y'all today?"

"We were wondering if we could speak with Paul Clapp," Gayle replied.

The woman glanced down at her desk calendar. "Is he expecting you?" she asked.

"No, we just need to ask him a few quick questions," I explained.

"It's about an employee ... Robin Day," Gayle added.

The woman cocked her head. "Are you police officers?" she asked. You could tell by the expression on her face that she didn't really think we were police officers, but was just making sure. I found it odd that her first thought was that police officers were here to question her boss.

"No," Gayle said. "We've been retained by her family."

"Oh. Give me one second." The woman got up from her desk, turned, and walked to a door a few feet behind her. She knocked briskly and went in.

We could hear muffled voice coming from inside the room, but couldn't understand what was being said. The woman returned a minute later. "You can go right in," she said.

We thanked her and went inside.

Paul Clapp was a very large man who really needed a bigger desk chair, because parts of him were hanging over the armrests of the one he had. Paul had greasy black hair that was parted on the side, and his double chin completely hid the collar of his white button-up dress shirt. The big roll of fat reminded me of a frog's inflatable vocal sac. He smiled nervously when we entered.

High Maintenance

"Good morning," Paul said. "Please have a seat."

Gayle and I sat down in the two chairs that faced him. "I'm Gayle Langley, and this is my husband Rex. We—"

Paul put up his hands. "Whatever she said about me was a lie," he protested. "I may have accidentally brushed up against Ms. Day, and maybe joked around a little, but I never insinuated that I was going to give her a raise."

"What are you talking about?" Gayle asked.

"Wait, what are *you* talking about?" asked Paul.

"We're talking about your missing employee," I said.

"Missing employee? Who?"

"Robin Day," said Gayle

"Missing from where?"

"Missing from everywhere," I said. "You haven't noticed?"

"How would I notice?" Paul asked. "She hasn't worked here in over two weeks."

Gayle and I looked at each other. "When was her last day of employment?" Gayle asked.

Paul pressed a button on his intercom. "Judy, when was Robin Day's last day of employment?"

"Hold on, Paul," came Judy's voice from the speaker.

"Judy will get that information for you," Paul said.

"Thanks," I responded.

"Did she quit?" Gayle asked. "Or was she fired?"

"Um ... we had a little disagreement," Paul answered, "and then she decided to seek employment elsewhere."

"Robin's last day was the ninth," Judy stated.

"Thank you, Judy," said Paul. He returned his attention to us. "There you go ... the ninth."

"Seventeen days ago," I said.

"A Monday," Gayle added. "Do you know if she found another job?"

"Oh, she already had another job," said Paul. "That was our main conflict. She got a part-time job a few months ago. She worked there every Tuesday and Friday. I voiced some concerns that it might interfere with her work here as a customer service rep. She assured me it wouldn't. But then a couple weeks ago she came to me and asked if she could drop down from full time to part-time here, so she could put in more hours at her other job. Seemed odd to me, because she could have a good future here, if she wanted it."

"Where was this other job?" Gayle asked.

"I'm not sure," said Paul. "She never actually said what she was doing. Or maybe she said, and I wasn't listening." Paul looked at me and added ingratiatingly, "You know how women are. On and on. You never know if you're supposed to be listening or not."

"Maybe she said something to Judy," I said.

Paul pressed the button again. "Judy, did Robin ever say anything to you about her other job?"

"No," Judy replied. "Not really. I think it had something to do with real estate or something. But she was never too specific."

Gayle leaned forward and pulled one of the many pencils out of the pencil holder on Paul's desk. I was a little nervous she was going to stick it in Clapp's eye for the "you know how women are" comment, but she just jotted down her name and number on a yellow Post-It note. She stuck it to the surface of Paul's desk. "Thanks,

Mr. Clapp," she said. "If you think of anything else, please, give us a call."

Paul shot Gayle a salacious grin. I half expected his double chin to inflate like a frog in heat. "You know I will, sweetheart," he crooned.

"And don't ever call me sweetheart again."

The smile quickly left Paul's face. Gayle was still holding the pencil, with the sharp end pointed in his direction.

"Yes, ma'am," said Paul.

We walked back out to the parking lot. "So she had another job," I commented.

"Every Tuesday and Friday," said Gayle.

"You think JB is her boss?"

"Seems that way." Gayle pulled out her cell and dialed. "I'm calling Trenton Boyd," she said. She put it on speaker.

"Hello?" said Boyd.

"It's Gayle Langley."

"Did you find her?" Boyd asked.

"Not yet," said Gayle. "Boyd, do you know anything about another job Robin had?"

"No, that's news to me. Who told you she had another job?"

"She worked at this job every Tuesday and Friday for last couple months. We think JB must have been her boss. It may have had something to do with real estate."

"I didn't know anything about that, but there were a few Fridays recently that I asked to see her and she said she had something going on."

"But she didn't say what that was?" Gayle asked.

"No."

"Okay, thanks." Gayle started to hang up.

"Wait," Boyd said.

"What is it?"

"The blackmail caller."

"Did they call back?"

"No, but the other day when your husband said the police might eventually speak with my wife, I decided to tell her about the affair."

"What did she say?"

"She said she already knew about it, and that it was her and a friend who pretended to be the blackmailers. She said she did it to scare me into breaking up with Robin."

"I guess it worked."

"Yeah, I guess it did."

"Call me if you think of anything else," Gayle said, and hung up. "Did you hear all that?"

"I heard."

"The wife knew about the affair."

"How do we know it wasn't Boyd's wife who had something to do with Robin's disappearance?"

"Good question, but if she did have something to do with it, I don't think she would have admitted to Boyd that she knew about the affair."

As we pulled out of the parking lot, Gayle's cell phone rang.

"Hello?" said Gayle. "Yes, this is Gayle. Yes, Sherri. The thirteenth of *this* month?"

I looked on as Gayle spoke. I liked it better when she put her cell on speaker.

"Will she still be there in an hour? Yes, just a few questions. Okay, Sherri, thank you. You too." Gayle hung up the phone and turned to me. "That was Sherri James, from Deena's Hair Salon."

"What did she have to say?"

"She said that Becky, one of her employees, came back to work today after a week off. Sherri told her about us coming into the salon asking about Robin. Becky reminded Sherri that Robin hadn't called to make her hair appointment that in fact she had stopped into the salon on the thirteenth and made the appointment for last Friday in person. Becky remembered Robin being there because she said it looked like Robin had been crying. When she asked Robin if she was okay, Robin replied that her boyfriend had broken up with her the night before."

"So Boyd was telling the truth," I said.

"About the breakup anyway."

"And now we're headed back to the salon?"

"Yeah. I want to speak with Becky myself."

Chapter Fifteen

We went straight to the hair salon ... by way of Dairy Queen. Gayle gave Sherri a little wave when we walked in. Sherri waved back, and then motioned to Becky, and Becky turned around.

"Hi," Gayle said. "You're Becky?"

"Yes," the young red head said, holding out her hand to shake. "Becky Lint."

The old sourpuss whose blue rinse Becky was giving a touch-up to glared into the mirror at Gayle.

"Gayle Langley," said Gayle, taking Becky's hand. "I understand Sherri already explained to you why we were here the other day."

"Yes."

"Sherri said you remembered speaking with Robin, and that it looked like she had been crying."

"Yes. Her eyes were red and all puffy. I asked her if everything was okay. She told me that her boyfriend had just broken up with her the night before, and that her car had broken down the same day and was in the shop. She said it was just one thing after another. I felt so bad for her."

The crabby old bat continued to stare and even let out a few sighs. Becky ignored her.

"Did she mention the boyfriend's name?" Gayle asked.

"No, but ..." Becky leaned in closer, and whispered. "But evidently he was married."

"I see," Gayle nodded. "We've also learned that Robin had quit her job the night before her boyfriend broke up with her. Did she say anything about that?"

"Hmm ..." Becky looked to the ceiling in thought. "I don't remember her saying anything about a new job, but she did say she was making some changes, and that this was going to be the start of a whole new life. So, I guess that could have meant she was starting a new job."

"Her appointment was for hair and nails, wasn't it?" I asked.

"Yes, it was," said Becky. She smiled, recalling their conversation. "She said she was really going to need the manicure after all the cleaning she was going to be doing."

"Cleaning?" Gayle asked. "Did she say *what* she was going to be cleaning?"

Becky shrugged. "I assumed it was her apartment or something."

"Did she say when the cleaning was supposed to take place?"

"Not that I recall." Becky turned back to her crabby customer and resumed applying the blue rinse.

High Maintenance

"It's about time," the old battle-axe said under her breath, but loud enough that everyone could hear.

"Thanks for your help, Becky," said Gayle. "If you think of anything else, Sherri has my number."

"Okay," said Becky.

Gayle turned to Sherri. "Also, Sherri, can I make an appointment to get these grays covered up? They're getting out of control."

I inconspicuously inspected Gayle's head as she spoke, wondering what gray hairs she was talking about.

Sherri turned and walked to the front desk. "You sure can," she said.

Gayle booked an appointment, Sherri thanked her, and the two of us headed for my truck. I wanted to ask Gayle about the gray hair, but I figured they were similar to the fat rolls she sometimes showed me—that I didn't see—and the nonexistent wrinkles she constantly complained about.

We climbed into my truck and headed down the street. We hadn't gone more than two blocks when Gayle's cell phone rang; it was the garage. Mike, our mechanic, said Gayle's car was finished, and that we could pick it up any time we liked.

"Thank God," Gayle said after hanging up. "That was rough being without a car."

"Sure it was," I said.

"What's that supposed to mean?"

"Nothing," I replied. "What do you think Robin was cleaning?"

"I wonder," Gayle replied.

"You think her new job was with a maid service, or something like that?"

"Maybe. But it seems odd that someone would leave a good job at an insurance company for a menial position like that."

"Maybe she was starting her own business," I offered.

This time it was my cell phone that rang. I looked at the call screen. "It's Rance," I said. "Should I let it go to voicemail?"

"Might as well get it over with."

"Hey, pal!" I said. "What's up?"

"Where are you?" Rance barked.

"Is something wrong?"

"Where are you?" he repeated. He sounded angry. I wished I had let it go to voicemail.

"Driving along Sadler Road."

"I got the fingerprint results back this morning."

"Oh, yeah? Cool."

"I phoned Trenton Boyd this morning to see if he knew or had heard of Robin Day."

"Oh, yeah?"

"You know what he told me?"

"I can't imagine."

"He said he already spoke with you and your wife!" Rance shouted. He was so loud I had to pull the phone away from my ear. Gayle's eyes widened, but she was smirking a little.

"Is that bad?" I asked.

"The police station ... now!" *Click!*

"He sounded kinda mad," Gayle observed.

"Yeah, he probably only had a salad for lunch."

High Maintenance

"And no caffeine," Gayle added.

"Poor guy really needs a burger."

Chapter Sixteen

"I'm sorry," I said. "We were just trying to help."

"Help who!" Rance hollered.

We were sitting in an interrogation room. I was disappointed; it was nothing like the ones from the film noirs I'd seen on Turner Classic Movies. No gooseneck lamp shining a 100-watt incandescent bulb in my face. No paint peeling off the cinder block walls. No rumpled detective spouting snappy dialogue at a machine-gun pace. The room was bright and neat—practically cozy. Gayle and I sat on one side of a six-foot table, and Detective Rance sat on the other. He had a legal pad in front of him with a pen lying next to it. Two large windows looked out over the squad room. Everyone out there looked over when Rance shouted.

"I don't know what you want me to say," I said.

Gayle jumped in. "We just thought we could ask around and find out where Robin went. There wasn't even an ongoing investigation, so we really didn't step on anyone's toes."

"Me being anyone," Rance pointed out.

"Well, yeah," Gayle responded. "But we figured as soon as we had something solid we would come to you. It wasn't our fault there was a mix-up with the fingerprint results."

"Yeah, mix up," Rance mumbled.

"Who knew we would get the results before you?"

"Yeah, who knew," said Rance. "Who else besides Trenton Boyd have you spoken with?"

"Sherri James," I said.

Rance started writing. "Who is Sherri James?" he asked.

"Robin's hairdresser," I said. "Over at Deena's Salon."

"Anyone else?"

"Becky Lint," Gayle said. "She also works at the salon."

"Is that it?"

"Paul Clapp," I said.

Rance kept jotting down names. "Paul Clapp is?"

"Robin's boss in Jacksonville," Gayle replied. "It's an insurance office on Dunn Avenue."

"Allstate," I added. "And there was the receptionist, Judy."

"That's everyone you spoke with?" Rance asked.

"And Trenton Boyd's mom," I said. "But that was just to get Boyd's phone number and address."

Rance put the pen tip on Sherri James' name. "We're going to go down this list and you're going to tell me everything each one of these people told you."

"Of course," Gayle said.

We stayed put for the next forty-five minutes and told Rance everything we knew about the disappearance of Robin Day. He had a lot of questions for us as well—some we knew the answers to, but most we didn't.

When we were finished, Rance asked, "Is there anything else you can think of?"

I shook my head. "Nope. I don't think so."

"That's it," Gayle said. "You know everything we know."

"If you need us for anything else, just give a shout," I said.

Rance glared at me. "I don't need you for anything."

"No," Gayle replied. "But everything you have there is the result of our legwork."

Rance shot her a look. "Get out," he said coldly. "And as far as the two of you are concerned, you're off the case."

We did as he ordered and hurried out of the police station.

As Gayle climbed into the passenger side of my truck she said, "Well, I guess we're off the case."

"Yup," I said. "I wonder what Robin was cleaning."

"*That's* the missing piece of the puzzle," Gayle replied.

I dropped Gayle off at the repair shop and then she drove over to pick up Stacy at school. By the time the two of them pulled into the driveway, I was sitting in Chester's driveway with him and Ho. We were halfway through our first bottle of beer.

"Hey, guys!" Stacy hollered.

"Hey, neighbor!" Chester hollered back. "Nice kid."

"Yes she is," I agreed.

"How long's she gonna be stayin' with y'all?" Ho asked.

"Not sure. As long as she wants, I guess."

"Gayle said the kid's old man is a miserable prick," said Chester.

"Yeah," I said. "I guess he's quite the boozer, and smacks her mom around a bit."

"Maybe we should pay him a visit some night," Chester suggested, "and give him a good old-fashion Southern attitude adjustment. Might just be what the ol' boy needs."

I grinned at the thought of layin' a boot upside George's ass. "If only it were that easy, Chester."

"Was a day it was that easy. Take it from me. I got firsthand knowledge of it."

"What do you mean?" I asked.

"Oh, this one time when I was about nine years old, my old man come home from a bender, and didn't like gettin' the third degree from my ma. They got into this big fight. They was screamin' an yellin' and I tried to break them up. My old man shoves me to the floor. Banged me up pretty good."

"Jeez," I said.

"That wasn't all," Chester continued. "He also gave my ma a black eye. The next day my ma tells my aunt about it. Later that night, my ma's three brothers pay us a visit. The upshot: my old man spent the next three days in the hospital."

"What happened after that?"

High Maintenance

"That was a turning point for my old man. He never took another drink after that night. He was a different person after that. I don't think I ever heard my old man raise his voice to my ma again, much less his hand. He was a good dad after that too."

"Wow, that's some story, Chester."

"I ain't sayin' something like that would change every man, but it worked on my old man."

We relaxed there quietly for a few minutes, and then Chester jumped up. "I need one more," he said. "How about you two?"

"I'm good," said Ho.

"Yeah, Chester, I'm good too," I said. "I better see what's going on over to my place."

I got up, and as I walked down Chester's driveway, I heard him say, "You keep that story in mind, Rex. Desperate times call for desperate measures."

I gave Chester a wave over my head and kept walking.

Chapter Seventeen

Gayle and Stacy were in the backyard with Vincent Van Gogh. I went out through the slider and joined them. Stacy was throwing a stick, and Vincent was chasing after it.

"Learn anything new today?" I asked.

"Probably," Stacy replied. "How about you?"

"Probably," I said.

"Cops hate when you butt in," Gayle whispered out of the side of her mouth.

"I *did* learn that."

"I learned something too," Gayle informed me.

"Oh yeah, what's that?"

"Robin Day uses the same mechanic as us."

"Mike?" I asked. "Seriously?"

"Yup. And Mike said that he worked on Robin's car on the twelfth."

"No kidding."

"And she was very concerned about getting her car back the next day, because she was starting a new job on the fourteenth. A job cleaning empty houses."

"So she was starting a new job. What about the part time-job she told her boss, Paul Clapp about? I thought she was increasing her hours at her part-time job."

"Maybe she was doing both. Think about it, back when you were doing construction, you started new jobs all the time. Maybe she was doing the same thing."

"Because I was self-employed."

"Exactly."

"And so was Robin Day."

"Exactly," said Gayle. "Mike also said the trunk of Robin's Kia was full of cleaning supplies."

"Which she would have to provide if she was self-employed," I said, finishing Gayle's thought.

We watched Stacy as she ran around the yard playing with Vincent. It was hard to tell who was having more fun: the dog, Stacy, or me for piecing clues together.

"So where do we go from here?" I asked.

"Judy at the Allstate office said Robin's job had something to do with real estate," said Gayle. "And Mike said it was a job cleaning empty houses."

"It started out being every Tuesday and Friday," I added, "but then increased as business picked up."

"I say we search the phone book for a real estate agent with the initials JB," Gayle said.

"Good idea," I said, and ran for the phone book. When I returned to the patio, I tossed the book on the patio table.

High Maintenance

Gayle looked down at the phone book and back at me. "Go ahead," she said. "I'm at the top of this investigative team. Looking through phone books is your job."

"Wow." I pulled out a chair, sat down, and began my search. It only took me a second to find James Blanchard Real Estate. "Bingo!" I said.

"That was quick," said Gayle.

"Yeah, maybe someday I'll be at the top of this investigative team."

Gayle laughed. "Keep dreaming."

"Gayle?" Stacy asked.

"Yeah?" Gayle said.

"I was thinking maybe I would go over and see my mom for a while tonight. She said my dad is working until ten."

"Of course, sweetheart. Whatever you want to do."

Stacy smiled. "Can y'all drop me off there in a half hour or so? She said she's making dinner for me."

"We sure can," I said. "We've got an errand to run anyway."

"We do?" said Gayle.

"Sure," I said. "And if you were really on top of this investigation team, you'd know what it is."

Chapter Eighteen

We dropped Stacy off at her house a little before four o'clock. I had called James Blanchard's office, so we knew it was open until five. We drove straight there after dropping Stacy off at the Dawes' place.

"How should we do this?" I asked, on our way to the real estate office.

"Do what?" Gayle asked.

"You know," I explained. "Should we do like a good cop, bad cop kinda thing?"

Gayle tried to hide her amusement when she looked over at me; she didn't try very hard. "Good cop, bad cop?" she asked.

"Yeah, you know, like on TV."

"Let's just be ourselves."

"Fine."

Blanchard's real estate office was located on Eighth Avenue in Fernandina Beach. It was in a small strip mall that housed about five other businesses, including a sneaker store, a place that made custom signs, and a dog bakery called Redbones.

We pulled into a spot right in front of Blanchard's. "Look," I said, pointing at the sign, "a dog bakery. Did you know we had a dog bakery right here in Fernandina Beach?"

"I had no reason at all to know that," Gayle replied.

"I guess we know now. I wonder what they have in there."

"I'm guessing baked goods for dogs."

"Huh. I wonder if Vincent would like something."

"We'll have to ask him."

"I think I'll stop in there after we talk to Blanchard."

"Yeah," Gayle said with a sigh, "we sure better."

I opened my door and climbed out of the truck. "What's the matter, you don't think he would like a cookie or something?"

"I just think it's foolish," Gayle replied, as we walked to Blanchard's door.

"I'll remember that next time you want some baked goodies."

"I'm not a dog."

"You're kinda acting like a female dog at the moment." I flashed her a grin.

"Wow, maybe I will be the bad cop."

We walked into Blanchard's office and looked around. There was a reception desk in front of us, but no one was sitting at it. The computer monitor on the desk was off. Behind us, in front of the windows was a matching leather couch and armchair. In front of the couch was a glass-top coffee table with a few real estate and do-it-yourself magazines scattered about.

A door behind the desk opened and a man in a suit backed through it carrying a large cardboard box. He turned around and was clearly startled to see us. "Oh!" he said. "Hey, didn't see you there. What can I do for you folks today?" He heaved the box on to the desk and reached out his hand to me. "James Blanchard."

I shook his hand and said, "Rex Langley, and this is my wife, Gayle."

"Pleasure to meet you," he said. "You folks in the market for a new home?"

"No," Gayle replied. "We're in the market for a young woman."

The smile left Blanchard's face. "A young woman? I don't understand."

"Robin Day," said Gayle.

"Don't even get me started," he said, pointing at the empty desk. "Alice has been out sick for the last two days. Meanwhile, Robin's a no-show. She tells me she wants the job full-time and—"

"What do you mean, 'no-show'?" Gayle asked.

"She never showed up," Blanchard said angrily. "She tells me she quit her other job and that she was coming to work for me full-time—that was over two weeks ago—but I haven't heard from her since. I tried calling her cell phone for a few days, but she wouldn't answer. I left messages, she wouldn't even call me back. I don't know, maybe her boss offered her more money to stay with him. Whatever. Now I'm scrambling to get these houses cleaned and ready to show. Alice comes down with the flu and—wait, who are you, and why are you looking for Robin?"

"Robin hasn't been seen or heard from since Wednesday the thirteenth," I said.

"We're working with her family to locate her," Gayle said.

"Holy crap," said Blanchard. "Two weeks? So you're saying she didn't just leave me high and dry?"

"No," I said.

"Do you know exactly what day you spoke with her last?" Gayle asked.

"Yes, I do," said Blanchard. "Come in my office."

Blanchard turned and went back through the open door; Gayle and I followed. He opened a date book on his desk and flipped through the pages.

"Right here," Blanchard said, pointing at Thursday the fourteenth. "I sent her to a place over on Diamond Street, in Yulee. It's a duplex."

"Did you hear from her at all after that?" Gayle asked.

"Yes." Blanchard pulled out his cell phone and tapped the screen a few times. "She texted me at 3:22 and said she was all finished cleaning. I texted back, telling her to lock up, and that I would see her in the morning. She texted back, *okay*."

"And that was it?" I asked.

"Yeah. She never showed up here the next morning. She was supposed to be here at nine."

"You have the address of the place in Yulee?" Gayle asked.

"Certainly," Blanchard replied, and jotted it down on a notepad. He ripped off the top sheet and handed it to Gayle.

"Do you know if Robin drove her own car that morning?" I asked.

"I would assume so. I don't know for sure."

"Did the place on Diamond sell?" I asked.

"Not yet," said Blanchard.

"How about the guy's name who owns the place?" Gayle asked.

"Oh yeah, sure, that's Eugene."

"Eugene what?" I asked.

"Gallon," said Blanchard. "Nice guy. A little weird."

"A little weird, how?" I asked.

"You know, just a little strange."

"But you sent Robin to his house anyway?" Gayle asked.

"I didn't say he was dangerous, just a little weird. I'm sure he's harmless."

"Yeah, I'm sure he is," said Gayle.

"Have you done business with Gallon before?" I asked.

"Yeah," Blanchard said. "I sold him a piece of property on Roses Bluff Road a couple years back … maybe five minutes from his duplex."

"What's on that property?" Gayle asked.

"Nothing really. A couple small shacks, and the previous owner left three or four storage containers."

"Is Gallon living in the duplex?" Gayle asked.

"Yeah, he lives on the right-hand side. But Robin was only cleaning the left side."

Gayle handed Blanchard back the piece of paper. "Here," she said, "write Gallon's name and number, if you don't mind."

"Not at all," said Blanchard. Gayle wrote her own phone number down on a different piece of paper and gave it to Blanchard. "If you think of anything else, give me a call," she said.

"Will do," said Blanchard. He reached toward an acrylic display stand on his desk. "Can't let y'all get away without giving you my card. Y'all call me if you ever just get so sick of your house you just can't stand it any longer. I'll put you in something nice." Smiling, he held out the business card between his thumb and forefinger. Awkwardly, Gayle refused to take it; politely, I did. "My website's on there. Office phone, home ph—"

"We'll keep that in mind, Mr. Blanchard," Gayle interrupted.

We got back in the truck and headed for Yulee.

"Ya know," I said, fingering Blanchard's fancy card, "maybe we should think about getting business cards. That way you—"

"Not now, Rex," she said. She reached into her purse and pulled out her chrome .38 snub-nosed revolver. She opened the cylinder, slowly spun it, and slapped it back into position.

"You didn't tell me to bring my gun," I said.

"Then hopefully you won't need it."

Chapter Nineteen

We pulled to the edge of Diamond Street, two houses down from Gallon's, and I shut off my engine. There was a yellow Volkswagen Bug in the driveway on the right side of the house. We'd discussed the particulars of Robin's disappearance during the fifteen-minute trip from Fernandina to Yulee. Gayle was convinced "weird" Eugene Gallon was involved.

"You think Gallon did something to her?" I asked.

"The last person to see someone alive, usually knows what happened to them," Gayle replied.

"Whoa! Isn't that jumping to an awful big conclusion?"

"Call it woman's intuition."

"Let's call it ex-cop's intuition." I started to open my door.

"Wait," Gayle said.

"Aren't we going to talk to him?" I asked.

"Let's give it a few minutes."

I checked my watch; it was 6:10. The sun was almost down and the sky was turning a beautiful shade of purple, with a tinge of red on the horizon. "I wonder how Stacy's doing."

"Good, I hope."

"She said George was working until ten."

"Yeah, I wanted to be back by then to pick her up."

"You think George is going to clean up his act?"

"No."

"He might need a good old-fashioned Southern attitude adjustment."

Gayle smiled. "Where did you hear that?"

"It was just something Chester told me."

I proceeded to tell Gayle the story from Chester's childhood, and how the attitude adjustment worked so well on his father.

"Sounds like Chester's story had a happy ending," said Gayle.

"Sounds like," I agreed.

Gayle pulled the piece of paper Blanchard had given her out of her pocketbook. "Maybe we better move things along. Back the truck up thirty yards or so."

I started the truck and backed it further down the street. Gayle took out her cell phone, dialed the number, and put it on speaker.

"Hello?" a man answered.

"Eugene Gallon?" Gayle asked.

"Yeah."

"We know what you did."

"Who is this?"

"We know what you did to Robin Day."

"Don't call me again, or I'll call the cops!" Gallon hung up.

"The old *I Know What You Did Last Summer* routine," I said. "That'll never work."

No sooner did I get the words out of my mouth than Gallon's front door opened. He stepped out onto the porch and looked up and down the street. Gayle and I ducked down and peeked over the dashboard.

"Never work, huh?" Gayle whispered.

Gallon stood there for a few seconds scanning the street. He stepped back into the house, and returned outside moments later carrying his car keys. He jumped into his Bug, backed out of his driveway, and sped down the street toward us. Gayle and I lay down in the seat as he passed by. I started my engine, made a U-turn, and followed.

We took a right on Benchmark Avenue, and then another right on Chester Road.

"He's headed to his property on Roses Bluff Road," Gayle commented.

At the two-mile point, there was a fork in the road. Gallon went right to stay on Roses Bluff, and Gayle told me to go left.

"Step on it!" she said.

No one had ever told me to step on it before. This investigating thing was getting more and more fun. I stepped on it. I took the next right and then the next one after that.

"Slow down," Gayle said.

I slowed to around thirty miles an hour. We surveyed the tree line for any sign of Gallon.

"Headlights," Gayle said, pointing just off the road on her side. "Pull over up here."

I pulled the truck off the road as far as I could and we got out.

Gayle reached back into the truck and pulled her gun out of her purse. "Come on," she said.

We walked back up the road about fifty yards and jumped a little ditch before heading into the woods. The sun had been down for about fifteen minutes, but it was still plenty light enough to see, even in the trees. Gayle turned a little north and I followed. Finally we came to the edge of a clearing and stopped.

About forty yards in front of us was a small eight by ten shed with a steel roof. The exterior walls of the shed were plywood. There was an old wooden door on the front, and a small single-sash window facing us. A light was on in the shed. There were no power lines anywhere so we knew the light must be coming from a candle or a lantern.

"What do you think he's doing in there?" Gayle asked.

"Probably lowering lotion in a basket into an old dry-well," I said. "It puts the lotion on—"

"Seriously?"

"Sorry."

About a hundred feet in front of the shack were three rusted storage containers. Two of the containers were small, only about twelve feet long, but a third container was huge and looked like one you would see stacked on a cargo ship. The largest container had a thick chain around the opening mechanism and was padlocked.

"What do you think he keeps in those storage containers?" I asked.

"Blanchard said the previous owner left them, so maybe nothing."

"Or maybe something."

We watched from the trees as Gallon exited the shed with a shovel in one hand and his lantern in the other.

"What's he doing?" I asked.

Gallon dropped the light on the ground and then jammed the pointed shovel into the dirt.

"Digging a hole," said Gayle. "Call Detective Rance."

I patted my pockets. "Shit! My phone is on the dashboard."

Gayle shot me a scolding stare.

"Sorry," I said.

Gayle took her own phone out of her pocket and handed it to me. "Here."

"I don't know his number."

"Well, how do you usually call him?"

"I just tap 'Rance' in my contacts."

"Whose number *do* you know?"

"Yours."

"That's not going to help."

"I'll call 911."

"That won't put us in touch with Rance."

"Do you have Chester's number?"

"Yes."

I scrolled through her contacts until I came to Chester, and dialed.

"Hello?" said Chester.

"Hey, Chester," I whispered. "It's Rex. I need—"

"Who?" Chester asked. "Speak up. I can hardly hear you."

"Chester, it's Rex," I said just a little louder.

"Why ya whisperin'?"

"I can't explain. I need you to look up the number for the Fernandina Police Department and give it to me."

"It's 911."

"No, Chester, I need the actual number."

"Hold on."

After what seemed like an eternity, Chester gave me the number and I made the call.

"Fernandina Police Department," said a female dispatcher. "How may I direct your call?"

"This is Rex Langley," I said. "I need to speak with Detective Calvin Rance."

"He's out of the building right now. Can I direct you to someone else?"

"Listen, lady," I explained. "This is a matter of life or death. I need you to give this message to Detective Rance immediately. We are two and a half miles out on Roses Bluff Road, in Yulee, and we think we have found the man who abducted Robin Day."

"Who's Robin Day?" asked the woman.

"I don't have time to explain," I responded. "Just give him the damn message. This is an emergency. Tell him it's Rex and Gayle Langley."

"I'll give him the message," she said with a sigh.

I hung up the cell and handed it back to Gayle.

"Is he on his way?"

"I hope so."

Gallon's hole was now two feet deep, and oddly enough, the length and width of a human body. He dropped the shovel on the ground next to him, picked up the lantern, and started walking toward the large container.

"I guess we're about to find out what's in there," said Gayle.

Gallon pulled a key out of his pocket, opened the padlock, and unwrapped the chain from the locking mechanism. He turned and scanned the area, making sure no one was watching. Gayle and I moved stealthily behind a tree trunk.

Gallon pulled one of the large metal doors open. It made a loud sound of scraping metal as it swung on the hinge. He took one more look around and then stepped into the container. A few minutes later he exited and walked back to his shack.

Gayle slipped her gun into her back pocket. "Let's go," she said.

The two of us ran across the field to the container. We peeked inside. It was dark so Gayle pulled out her cell phone and tapped the screen, trying to give us some light. It smelled bad inside the container. Gayle put her hand over her nose. "Oh my God," she said.

"Help me," we heard someone whisper.

"Robin?" I asked.

"Please, help me."

We moved further into the container as Gayle shined her cell phone around trying to see. Our eyes were adjusting to the darkness, and I was starting to make out shapes.

"Robin?" Gayle said.

"Yes," the voice said. "Please hurry … before he comes back."

Robin Day was sitting in the back corner of the container. One of her wrists and one of her ankles were shackled to the side of the container. I crouched down and pulled on the chains.

"He has the key," Robin said.

I stood back up. "We have to get that key," I said.

"What about the other two girls?" Robin asked.

"What other two girls?" Gayle asked.

"There were two others," said Robin. "They were in here with me until yesterday."

"We didn't see anyone else," I said.

Just then the door swung shut. The metal on metal boom when it closed was deafening. I ran toward the door and pounded my fists. "Open the door!" I shouted. I could hear Gallon weaving the chain through the lock as I shouted. "We have a cell phone in here!" I pounded on the door a few more times. "We can just call for help, asshole!" I slammed the palm of my hand against the door.

"Rex!" Gayle shouted.

I turned. "What?"

"It's no use. Stop pounding on the door."

"Call 911," I said.

Gayle looked at her cell. "I'm not getting any service in here."

Chapter Twenty

Gayle and I huddled with Robin in the gloom of the pitch-black unit, comforting the poor girl. She told us the full story of her abduction and captivity.

It was a good hour before we heard someone knock on the end of the container and call out our names; it was Detective Rence.

"Rance, we're in here!" I called out. I felt my way back to the door and knocked. "Rance!"

"Rex, is that you?" he asked.

"Yes," I said.

"Let me find something to break this lock."

"Hurry up, and watch out for Gallon."

A few minutes later Rance was hitting the padlock with something. He hit four or five times, then I heard the chain being pulled through the lock. The door swung open. Now that the sun had fully set the container stayed dark even with the door open.

"Hey, pal," I said.

"Who locked you in here?" Rance asked.

"It was a guy named Eugene Gallon. Robin Day was cleaning a house he was selling." I turned and pointed back at Robin. "She's alive," I said.

Rance tried to see past me, but could see only darkness. "Is Gayle with you?"

"Yes," I said. "Did you find Gallon? He was in that shack."

"I looked inside but there wasn't anyone in there." Rance pulled out his cell phone to call for backup.

"Was there still a Volkswagen Bug out by the road when you came in?"

"Yeah, it was out there, but—"

A shot rang out and Rance fell sideways against the open door.

"Holy shit!" I shouted, and jumped back.

Rance rolled to his back and looked up at me. He was holding his shoulder. I squatted down next to him and grabbed his shirt, trying to pull him into the container for cover.

I looked up to my left to see Gallon standing above us. Gallon pointed his pistol and I threw myself onto Rance. I shut my eyes tightly and waited for the shot.

Bang!

I didn't feel anything. I wondered if Gallon had missed. I froze, waiting for him to fire again.

"Get off me," Rance said.

I opened my eyes and looked where Gallon had been standing; he wasn't there. He was lying on his back in the dirt a few feet away from us.

I jumped up and turned toward Gayle and Robin. Gayle was walking to the front of the container, her .38 in her hand.

"Nice shot," said Rance.

I walked over to Gallon and searched the ground for his weapon. He turned his head and looked at me and moaned.

I found Gallon's gun, picked it up, and trained it on his face. "Where're the other two girls?" I bellowed.

Gallon smiled. "I already buried them," he said. "You'll never find them."

I pulled back the hammer.

"Don't do it," Rance said.

I thought about it. I wanted more than anything to put a bullet in Gallon's head.

"Don't, Rex," Rance said again. "He's not worth it."

Gayle put her hand on mine and gently pulled my hand down. I released the hammer and she took the gun from me.

"Where're the keys to those chains, Gallon?" Gayle demanded.

Gallon still had his eerie grin. "In my front pocket, sweet thing," he said. "Why don't you reach in there and get them?"

"Don't mind if I do," said Gayle, and she kicked him in the head, knocking him unconscious.

Gayle put her .38 back in her back pocket and retrieved the keys. She walked back into the container and unlocked Robin from her shackles, as I helped Rance to his feet.

"I can't believe you threw yourself on me, you idiot," Rance said.

"That's what pals do," I said.

Gayle helped Robin to the door and the young woman stepped into freedom for the first time in two weeks. As she walked past Gallon's unmoving body, her face broke into a grimace. "D-dead?" she whispered.

"Sorry, no," Gayle replied.

Rance had just gotten off his cell. He directed his remarks to Robin. "Ambulances are on the way, miss. One for you and me, and one for that piece of shit. Pardon my French. Looks like he'll pull through. And he'll be going to jail for a long, long time." Rance turned to Gayle and me. "It pains me to say this, but you two did right good work."

"Thanks, pal," I beamed.

"For amateurs," he added pointedly. "Next time do me a favor."

"What?" Gayle and I said together.

"Don't let there be a next time."

Chapter Twenty-One

It was almost ten o'clock by the time we left Gallon's property and headed back to Fernandina Beach.

"Maybe you better give Stacy a call and let her know we're on our way," I said.

"I already tried," Gayle said. "My cell is dead. Can you call her?"

"I don't know her number."

"Of course you don't."

"You want me to call Chester and have him—"

"No. We won't be that late anyway."

It was around ten-thirty when we rounded the corner onto Eleventh Street. We saw the flashing lights immediately. There was a Fernandina patrol car blocking the street and a Nassau County Sheriff's car at the edge of the street. There were several other police cars on the street as well, all with their light bars flashing. Two ambulances sat parked in front of George and Libby's place.

"No, no," Gayle said as we drove up.

I pulled my truck to the curb. Gayle was out of the truck and running for the house before I had come to a complete stop. I shoved the shifter into park and ran after her.

"Gayle!" I shouted. "Wait!"

An officer put up his hands to stop her, but she was too quick. She ducked and dodged him. "Ma'am, you can't go in there!" he hollered.

As the officer's attention was on Gayle, I ran around him.

As I neared the house, two paramedics wheeled a body bag, on a gurney, out the front door.

Gayle froze in horror.

George Dawes appeared in the doorway, bleary-eyed and disheveled. His expression was at once incredulous and insolent. His hands were cuffed behind his back. An officer nudged him none too gently through the opening. George pitched forward, caught his balance, and staggered down the concrete walkway.

Gayle ran past the gurney and leapt into the air. "What did you do!" she screamed. She landed on George, and George stumbled backwards onto the concrete.

Gayle hit him with a right, and a left, and another right. "What did you do!" George yelped in meek protest as the blows rained down upon his head and face.

A second officer ran to help. They grabbed Gayle's arms but she continued to swing.

"Stop!" one of the officers shouted.

"Who is it?" I asked one of the paramedics. "Who is it?"

They both just looked at me like I was crazy.

"Who's in the body bag!"

"Rex!" someone behind me yelled.

I turned, and so did Gayle. It was Stacy. I ran to her and dropped to my knees in front of her. "Are you okay?"

"I'm okay ... but, my mom—"

"I know," I said.

"He came home drunk," said Stacy.

Gayle finally made it to us and threw her arms around the young girl. "It's going to be okay," she said. "It's going to be okay," she murmured.

Gayle and Stacy sobbed, and I wiped the tears from my eyes with the back of my hand. I stood and turned around. The two officers were putting George into the back of one of the patrol cars. That made twice in one night that I wanted more than anything in the world to kill someone.

George Dawes sat in the patrol car slumped over and staring into his lap. He was going to be sorry when he sobered up, just like he always was, but this time it would be too late. As I stared at him through the window, I wondered if a good old-fashioned Southern attitude adjustment would have helped.

The End

Coming Soon:

Excited About Nothing
Jake Stellar Series

ALSO BY RODNEY RIESEL

From the Tales of Dan Coast Series

Sleeping Dogs Lie
Ocean Floors
The Coast of Christmas Past
Ship of Fools
Double Trouble
Most Likely to Die
Deadly Moves
On the Wagon
No Enemies Here

Jake Stellar Series

North Murder Beach
Beach Shoot
When Death Returns
The Obedience of Fools
Dead in the Water

The Dunquin Cove Series

The Man in Room Number Four
Return to Dunquin Cove
Local Hero

Sunrise City Series
Sunrise City
Sunrise City 2: From Bad to Worse
Never Strikes Twice

Fernandina Beach Mysteries
Maintenance Required

From Here to There: A Collection of Short Stories